Greenwoman

A Literary Garden of . . .

Fiction ❋ Nonfiction ❋ Poetry ❋ Commentary

Biography ❋ Art ❋ Comics

**Volume Three -
The Victory of Dirt**

Editor-In-Chief: Sandra Knauf
Deputy Editor: Zora Knauf
Copy Editor and Brilliant-Advisor-on-
Everything-Else: Cheri Colburn

Chief Designer: Sandra Knauf
Web Designer/Tech. Support: Paul Spielman

Advertising contact: Sandra Knauf
(719) 473-9237
sandra@greenwomanmagazine.com

Attn. retailers: For more information about
selling this marvelous magazine in your store
call 719-473-9237 or write
sandra@greenwomanmagazine.com

ISBN-10: 0989705668
ISBN-13: 978-0-9897056-6-0

*www.greenwomanmagazine.com
www.florasforum.com
www.zeraandthegreenman.com
www.greenwomanpublishing.com
www.gardenshorts.com*

Send comments, questions, concerns, and
brilliant submissions of art and writing to:
Greenwoman Magazine, PO Box 6587,
Colorado Springs, CO 80934-6587

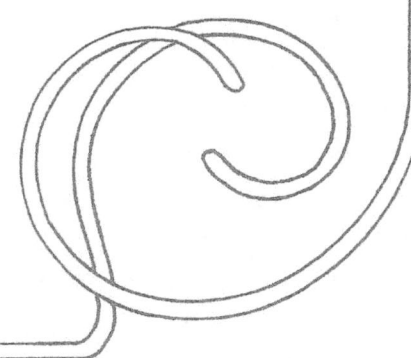

Contents

Front cover art *"Pip Flora"* by Nadine Sage.

Editor's Letter

The best of times, the worst of times. Dickens' words seem especially appropriate when looking at today's agriculture and gardening. The bad news? More than ever, multinationals have a choke-hold on our food system and our lives. The good? (And by *good* I mean very, very good.) We're making big changes, claiming our independence by learning, sharing, *doing*; and it feels *great*.

Creating change isn't easy though, and the best effort is in-person effort. If you believe a political candidate truly represents you, put on your walking shoes and help her—in person. If our food supply is at the top of your concerns, start a garden club, join a CSA or a group on raising chickens. We can also "vote" every day—with our dollars and our actions. Now is the time to start that vegetable garden, orchard, or pond, build that chicken coop or bee hive, meet your local organic farmer and become a customer. Make your voice heard online by contacting your elected officials and showing them you're serious about making this world a better place.

As you'll see in *Greenwoman*'s third volume, these changes infuse our literature and art. Probably our most notable offering along these lines is an excerpt from Joel Salatin's book *Folks, This Ain't Normal: A Farmer's Advice for Happier Hens, Healthier People, and a Better World. Folks* was the first book I read in 2012 and I knew immediately it would be the most important book I would read that year. It is *brilliant*.

Salatin, who first came on the national pop culture radar through Michael Pollan's *Omnivore's Dilemma*, has also appeared in the films *Food, Inc.* and *Fresh*. I had read some of Salatin's work and thought it was exclusively about farming. Not anymore. His latest book goes to the heart of everything that's important about American food. All of Joel's wisdom is distilled in some very fine writing directed to the scale of the individual—from apartment dweller to backyard food producer.

I'm also excited about LaManda Joy's piece on the history of WWII Victory Gardens. I found Joy last year while blog-surfing and asked if she'd share her considerable knowledge on the subject with our readers. Her intriguing article will teach you lot about an era where people grew their own food. The message is simple: They did it, so can we.

Other thrills include art from my dear and talented friend Paul Spielman who illustrated Salatin's story with *the* perfect drawing, and a new artist I discovered on Etsy, Laura Chilson. Chilson created two big last minute projects for this volume, illustrations for *Mr. Stripey (A Tragedy)* and *The Gardener's Dirty Mind*. Only after we began corresponding did I learn that she is also an avid gardener (turning over the soil in her brand new vegetable/herb patch this May in her rented home) and that she also works as a landscaper.

There are many more highlights: Elisabeth Kinsey's piece on dirt, Dan Murphy's nature wisdom, Simone Martel's terrific "Almost Too Happy," and some amazing poetry. I am personally wild about every contribution. My fondness and gratitude for the authors and artists who have made this volume possible is immense.

Here's a toast to us all. To enjoying a fertile, rambunctious, thoughtful, and abundant growing and harvest season—both in and out of the garden.

Sandra

Sandra Knauf'
Editor and Publisher

Zora Knauf,
Deputy Editor
Extraordinaire

Contributors

Michael Andreoni's stories have appeared in *Euphony*, *Pif Magazine*, *Iconoclast*, *Thumbnail*, *EFiction*, and other publications. He lives near Ann Arbor, Michigan. He had no picture available and so described himself thus: "I have lovely appendages and there is a certain amount of hair. My head has been described as 'Leonine' by someone I suspect has never seen a lion. The wife likes to imitate my duck-footed walk when she's peeved at me, though my craggy Italian nose is beyond her talents. I have the pores of a god."

Born in Rochester, NY, **Laura Chilson** graduated with her BFA from SUNY Purchase School of Art+Design in 2008. She currently resides in Ithaca, NY. Specializing in pencil portraits and oil paintings, she can be reached through her website, www.LauraChilson.com.

Cheri Colburn is a writer, editor, and gardener who lives, works, and raises human beings in Colorado Springs, Colorado. Her "likes" include hiking, the sound of her children's voices, and long days digging in the dirt. Her "dislikes" include dieting, deadlines, and quitting bad habits.

Cheryl Conklin is a landscape gardener, writer, and educator lucky enough to have followed her bliss. You can see more of her work, find contact information, and link to her blog at http://www. greenwaygardening.com.

LaManda Joy is an award-winning Master Gardener, author of the popular urban gardening blog "The Yarden," a Square Foot Gardening™ Certified Instructor, and founder of The Peterson Garden Project, a community and edible garden education program in Chicago, Illinois. She is a board member of the American Community Gardening Association, member of The Culinary Historians of Chicago, and a national speaker on Victory Gardens and other edible garden topics. Her lecture at the Library of Congress can be seen at www.youtube.com/watch?v=fXeLqmsPf6U

Pat Kennelly is a freelance writer, poet and gardener who lives and works in Colorado Springs, Colorado. Most recently her work has appeared in *The Denver Post*, *Haibun Today*, *Articus* and *Messages from the Hidden Lake*.

Elisabeth Kinsey teaches writing online, lives in Denver, pines away for Half Moon Bay and publishes in *The Denver Post* and various journals. Her hands are imminently dirty. She may or may not be related to the late Dr. Alfred Kinsey.

Contributors

Jane Knechtel has worked as a psychotherapist and serves on the Board of Directors of *In Other Words* Feminist Community Center in Portland, Oregon, one of nine remaining feminist bookstores left in the country (there were over 200 in 1980). Her work has appeared or is forthcoming in *The Sunday Oregonian*, *The Tar Wolf Review*, *Reed: A Journal of Poetry & Prose*, *Fire* (U.K.), *Woman Made Gallery*, *The Tusculum Review*, and others. Her many honors and awards include the 2006 Parnell Prize in Poetry and the 2008 Donn Goodwin Poetry Prize.

Kathryn Kulpa is the author of the story collection *Pleasant Drugs* (Mid-List Press) and has published work recently in *Monkeybicycle*, *Northville Review*, *Metazen* and *Foundling Review*. She is the editor of *Newport Review*, a literary e-zine. She lives in New England and is apt to rescue cats.

Janae Lehto is a colored pencil, charcoal, and pastel artist specializing in nature and animals. She has shown in several galleries around North Carolina and is an active member of local and national art guilds. Her work can be found in private art collections throughout the U. S. and abroad.

Simone Martel is the author of *The Expectant Gardener*. Her stories have appeared in many publications including *Greenprints*, *Magnolia* (with an excerpt on the podcast *One World Cafe*), and *Fantastique Unfettered*, (Pushcart nominated). She lives and gardens in Berkeley, CA, where she supports herself editing cookbooks and self-help books.

Gayla Mills lives in Richmond, VA, where she teaches writing at Randolph-Macon College. She has published essays, features, reviews, and short fiction. She completed her walkway, garden beds, and related backyard projects in three weeks without lasting injury to her body or relationships.

Dan Murphy is a seasoned zine writer (*The Juniper*, *Elephant Mess*) and proponent of the slow life. His long-time passions include bike riding, skateboarding, punk rock, and gardening. His new interests include botany, ecology, wildflowers, and lichens. Dan has a B.S. in horticulture and an M.S. in biology (his thesis was on green roof technology research). He works at the Idaho Botanical Garden in Native Plant Horticulture. www.juniperbug.blogspot.com

Patricia K. Nolan says, "I've long imagined retiring someday as Miss Rumphius and living in a meadow full of lupine. Until then, my 'urban farm' grows in containers on my townhouse patio, while I wait for the wisteria to bloom."

Contributors

Judith Offer has had two daughters, five books of poetry, and dozens of plays. (Eighteen of the latter, including six musicals, have been produced.) Her work has been included in the Library of Congress series and on NPR's "All Things Considered." Her most recent book of poetry, *Double Crossing*, is poems about Oakland, California where she lives with her husband, Stuart. www.JudithOffer.com

Rancher/writer **Tom Preble** lives in his self-built, earth-bermed and energy-efficient home and ranch on the Palmer Divide east of Colorado Springs. Something of a Renaissance man, Tom has wide ranging interests from astronomy to welding to philosophy. Trained as a computer electronics engineer and now semi-retired, Tom drives a school bus over the backroads of the Colorado prairie and observes and writes about his little friends on the bus. www.tompreble.com/

Bruce Holland Rogers writes very short stories in Eugene, Oregon, or wherever he happens to be living at the moment. In recent years he has temporarily resided in Budapest, London, and Toronto. He's hoping to spend three months researching stories in Japan in 2013. Rogers teaches fiction in the MFA program of the Northwest Institute of Literary Arts. www.shortshortshort.com.

At age 20, **Cynthia Rosi** emigrated from Seattle to London, determined to write for a living and to marry the Anglo-Italian boy she'd met at a bus stop during a University exchange program. They spent many happy summers in Tuscany, and Cynthia loved apprenticing in her husband's aunt's kitchen. Her daughter has followed in those footsteps, and learned last summer how to make home-made ravioli. Aunty Mabu inspired Cynthia's garden, her flock of chickens, and her best meals. www.simplyhugyourself.com

DB Rudin is an environmental education consultant, elementary school teacher, and the Education Coordinator at Venetucci Farm, an 190-acre historic farm in Colorado Springs, Colorado. He offers programs through Colorado Critter Encounters, which includes hands-on programs for kids on nature and conservation, and a class for those who tend the soil, The Good, the Bad and the Beautiful: Bugs 101 for Gardeners. www.cocritterencounters.com

Nadine Sage (this issue's cover artist) is a papier collé and oil artist. Encouraging a renewed appreciation for master illustrators of the past, Nadine infuses the past with the present. She integrates 18th and 19th century illustrations and imagery with contemporary decorative components and oil pastels. Collage never looked so good. www.sageandleo.com

Joel Salatin is a third-generation family farmer working his land in Virginia's Shenadoah Valley with his mother, Lucille, wife, Teresa, daughter, Rachel, son, Daniel, daughter-in-law, Sheri, grandsons, Travis and Andrew, and granddaughter, Lauryn, along with a cadre of employees, subcontractors, apprentices, and interns. Their Polyface Farm, a beyond organic grass-fed farm, services more than 4,000 families, ten retail outlets, and fifty restaurants through on-farm sales and metropolitan buying clubs. Joel Salatin writes extensively in magazine such as *Stockman Grass Farmer* and *Acres USA*.

Contributors

Marian Kaplun Shapiro, four-times Senior Poet Laureate of Massachusetts, is the author of a professional book, many journal articles, over 200 published poems, and three books of poetry. She practices as a psychologist in Lexington, Massachusetts.

Paul Spielman says he is a long-time coffee-house sketcher, doodler, Arch-Top electric guitar player, and genuine Art-School graduate (who was lucky enough to study under Ron Lucas); but mostly he is a puzzled people watcher. He makes his home in Colorado Springs, Colorado with his wife Sri, who is an artist and florist.

Larry Stebbins is the founder and director of Pikes Peak Urban Gardens, a botanist, and a retired science teacher. He has over 40 years experience as a biodynamic and organic gardener.

Rhonda Van Pelt is a journalism veteran, most recently writing about art, theater, and nonprofits for the *Colorado Springs Independent*. Rhonda tries to do something creative every day, and she enjoys celebrating nature through her photography and quilts.
Visit her website at www.rhondashouseofcreativity.shutterfly.com/

Carolyn Williams-Noren's poems have appeared in *Spoon River Poetry Review*, *Literary Mama*, and elsewhere. Her poem "Mistakes" received a 2009 Pushcart Prize nomination from *Seems*, and in 2010 E. Ethelbert Miller and Kristin Naca selected her work for a Loft Mentor Award. She lives and gardens in Minneapolis with her husband and two daughters, and misses the Oregon coast, where she was first entranced by blackberries.

Joe Wirtheim designs the "The Victory Garden of Tomorrow" poster campaign. He is a lifetime student of history and communication arts. Originally from Dayton, Ohio, he now lives, bikes, and eats in Portland, Oregon.

A Life Unplugged

I wanted to find a way to shed some of the anxiety brought on by modern life. The stresses of academia and the fears about what would come next were really wearing on me. I was filled with worry and burdened by the responsibilities of adulthood. I was having way too many unhealthy and unconstructive thoughts; it was getting kind of scary to tell you the truth. I didn't want my synapses to fire that way too consistently for fear that they would form habitual states of mind, resulting in my becoming perpetually paranoid and pessimistic. I wanted to feel free again. Young. Carefree. Innocent. But my body was breaking down, and I couldn't continue to deny my age or experience any longer. Nothing is simple anymore. Nothing is easy. There had to be a way to get through this without going completely berserk and off my rocker. Would I find it?

Have you ever unplugged yourself and walked out into the woods, shirking all responsibility and disarming yourself of modern day technology and 21st century conveniences? Has it ever been just you and the trees? Pull the earphones out of your ears. Turn off the cell phone. Get far enough away that you can no longer hear the roar of passing cars and the buzz of pedestrian traffic. It's just you. You and the sky. You and the birds. You and the lichens. Find a rotting log to rest upon. Sit there for a minute or two. Take some deep breaths. Forget about time. Forget about responsibility. Forget about deadlines and the never-ending to-do list. Right now it's just you and the insects. You and the understory herbaceous community. You and nature.

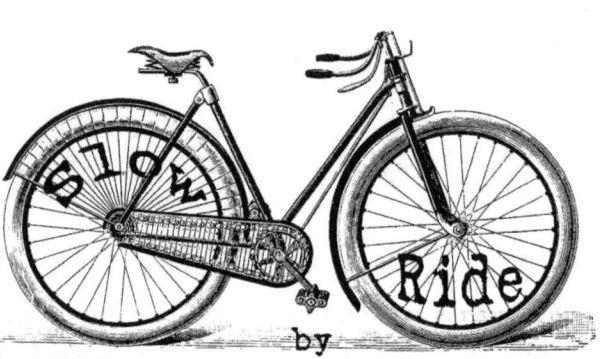

by **Dan Murphy**

Are we debunking materialism and our persistent over-consumption?

Considering that many of the things we see around us, both structurally and socially, are just constructs of mankind, you might think that it would be easy to just rise above it all or switch it all off. It's just a façade, after all—a figment of our imaginations, a silly mark of our engineering and electioneering prowess. Yet, there is a strong sense of permanence in our various and sundry constructions, and unfortunately they can not be shrugged off so easily. After all, we are the creators, the visionaries. We are the engineers. These constructs, whether bogus theories or tangible creations (and including their poisonous and resource-depleting aftermaths), are the result of our species. Even if we personally did not have a direct hand in creating them, the memes from which they emerged are the basis of our cultural conditioning, and we have been bathing in them since birth. We were born into this, even if we say to ourselves that we never would have chosen this. We all have to deal with the consequences of every collective choice our species has ever made throughout the entire duration of its existence. And now, we—the current generations—must select and manage the world our progeny will inherit and the existence that they will face. Do we fully understand the weight of this responsibility? Are we doing all we can to make improvements and innovations for our offspring in order to make their lives more pleasurable and sustainable? Are we debunking materialism and our persistent over-consumption? Are we leaving our youth with a healthy and properly functioning planet and the know-how to keep it that way? Or are we leaving them doomed? Will future generations look back on this era and be ashamed or proud? Will we evolve for the better . . . or for the worse?

I wanted to get away for a minute or two. I wanted to find a little peace among what I perceived as sheer insanity. I wasn't necessarily seeking answers, but I may have found some. That's what happens when you reconnect with nature. That's the result of spending time with your better half. We evolved from the same stuff that exists all around us: the stuff of plants and insects and mammals and trees. We are nature formed from star stuff. So can we learn to live like other creatures and create no waste? Can we find a way to move and act with greater simplicity? It seems like the answers must be out there, if only more of us were smart enough and brave enough and intuitive enough to go out and find them. Unplug. Quiet down. Listen. With patience and our trademark (and innately human) innovation, the answers will surely come. We just need a little perspective—perspective that, thankfully enough, only nature can provide. ✿

Blackberry Bramble
by Carolyn Williams-Noren

I've waited all year for this. Come
here. Come and take this. Set the pail
down. Now—over here. See? So
ready for you. One more
step in. See these? Oh—
Do that again. Show me
your lips again, and that
tongue. And give me your
wrist. Inside, you are so much
like me. Look at that ripeness
weeping out! Don't mind that. Here—
another one, so swollen
it will explode the moment
it feels your soft mouth, that mouth
like the clouds I've been arching
for all summer. All I want
is for us to be inside each other. Stay
and let me line your skin.
Stay and take me in. Cram
yourself full and I will ride
all day in the whorls
of your thumbprints, and in one
seed of moss and tea between
your teeth, and I will ease
my way beneath your sandal strap
and taste another morsel
of your salty jam
with every step.

Did you really think the pleasure
was only yours?
Don't you know
the purple rounds
of your fingertips
burn in my mind
all night while I toss
and turn in the foxglove,
trying to rest?

Collage by Angus Skillet

Mr. Stripey (A Tragedy)
by Michael Andreoni

Illustration by Laura Chilson

She has forgiven me. November's rain seemed a proper backdrop for apology as day by day the garden sank into sodden unfamiliarity. With the now-wooden asparagus cut off at the knees and the last of the lettuce frost-bit, it was no longer our green-tangled corner of contention. Oak leaves shrouded the vegetable beds in brown until, looking out from the living-room window, it was difficult to make out that a garden lived there. I could speak the words then, even if I did not completely believe in them, that everything had been my fault. My wife's loving embrace could not entirely erase my suspicions though, and now, as December shadows lengthen, there's plenty of time to look forward to next year.

We were so happy gardening side by side those first butterscotch-hued mornings of true spring. Raking winter-blasted decay from the vegetable beds, smoothing the soil, and smiling at partially disrobed earthworms undulating a brazen strip-tease, so appropriate to the season of rebirth. I watched Shelley watching them, grateful for her, the memory of cold already slipping away.

The thought of the garden coming between us was not for those days of promise, when every green shoot was our shared triumph. We planted summer's bounty in beds guarded by waving rows of daffodil sentries. Lettuce and broccoli under the trees where the sun was not so fierce, the tomatoes and peppers left fully exposed, ready to contest mid-summer heat with their own fiery glow. Sun on our backs, we laughed at the sweet irony of being too warm after months of wishing for just that.

Some seeds root only in winter's depths though, in the long, idle evenings of too many magazines and movies. I remember the moment last winter—snow blowing past the windows under failing light, Shelley napping in her chair—when I first saw the photo in a catalog. My

I'd like to think there was a struggle before I gave in to temptation.

hands immediately began shaking until I had to take a breath and wait for them to settle. It felt as though in my fifty-year-old, middle-aged life, I had never really lived, but now might begin.

"Rude health" was my first awkward attempt at describing Mr. Stripey, along with "rosy-cheeked," another quaint phrase that fit perfectly. So unapologetically beautiful, yet with a firm maturity that balanced a well-rounded form. Obviously bred for the camera, he nevertheless appeared unconscious of its caress, the lovely bending of light around him. His smooth-skinned innocence inspired desires that I hadn't felt in years.

I'd like to think there was a struggle before I gave in to temptation. Certainly there were thoughts of other tomatoes we'd tried in the past, all the tempting varieties that never quite fulfilled their promise when seed hit soil. I want to believe I considered these issues for a time before obsession swept all reason away. Some interval when I wavered in a space between the thinking and the doing. Probably that hesitation was never real until now, as laughable self-deception. I had seen the photo, and I could not have pretended indifference.

That my wife should be consulted was, I felt, a necessary, if daunting reality. Shelley reserved her most cutting disdain for the multi-colored, new-fangled varieties. She was strictly meat-and-potatoes regarding tomatoes, but maybe if she gazed upon Mr. Stripey's most noble form, read the seed catalogs glowing testimonials, it might be done.

"Mr. Stripey is our destiny," I began on a cold February evening.

"Yours, maybe."

She barely glanced at the photo before handing it back with the humoring half smile that usually stopped me quicker than arguing.

"No, really. We're both modern, experienced people. We can choose to have this in our lives. Mr. Stripey is for both of us."

"Disgusting."

I held the photo up. "Why is it disgusting? Can you look at this and tell me you're not attracted?"

She turned her face away. "You know I can't stand striped varieties. It's obscene."

So far everything adhered to the plan. My wife had behaved predictably—I could have guessed everything she'd said. I put that picture away and brought out another.

The second photo showed Mr. Stripey cut open to display the delectable red, yellow and orange flesh that I knew she would not be able to resist.

"Ugh! Get it away from me!"

"Isn't that a great tomato?"

"No!"

A struggle was to be expected. This was something beyond anything I'd ever asked of her. Still, I was surprised at the force behind her rejection.

"Why don't you like it?"

"The way it looks . . . the name . . . I hate that name, Mr. Stripey. It sounds too much like rough trade . . . like a street hustler.

"But you like Big Beef," I reminded her.

"Big Beef's been around forever."

"And Lemon Boy. Talk about rough trade, I've seen you eat a whole plate of Lemon Boy. And Early Girl; you can't get enough of that one. Or would you like to talk about last year's favorite: Dark Prince?"

Her smile came back. "I'm not going to argue with you. We're not having Mr. Stripey"

"Beefmaster. Early and Often."

"You can sit here and fantasize," She remarked on the way out of the living-room. "I'm going to bed."

"Ripe and Luscious!"

"You made that one up."

I had.

I kept trying throughout March and April, hoping she just needed a little more space to consider it. Each new attempt brought only a stronger denial and, with warm spring weather beckoning, I decided it wasn't worth pursuing Mr. Stripey any longer. I still had the photo. That would have to be enough.

It was after the broccoli was planted that my thoughts changed. We were walking along, discussing the new spot for the peppers, and reminding each other to keep the squash away from the cantaloupes. Shelley began laying out the tomatoes—Beefmaster here, Lemon Boy over there, with a few remarks thrown in about how much more space they had now that the

I'd heard a gloating tone in her voice, as though each name, Dark Prince, Early and Often, Big Beef, was really meant as Plenty Of Space For The Ones I like, But None For Mr. Stripey. Never, Ever, for Mr. Stripey!

peppers would no longer crowd them—when everything I'd tried to forget came back. How could she be so callous? I'd heard a gloating tone in her voice, as though each name, Dark Prince, Early and Often, Big Beef, was really meant as Plenty Of Space For The Ones I like, But None For Mr. Stripey. Never, Ever, For Mr. Stripey! She gave me that little victorius smile when I frowned, my loving wife, before moving on to radishes.

I didn't deserve it. It's one thing to win but quite something else to spike the ball. I had put Mr. Stripey aside for the sake of harmony, and my forbearance had been interpreted as weakness, an imprint of complete subjugation. She continued on, pronouncing confidently about this and that, unaware that a poor son of the soil had become restless. Slinking behind like a proper serf, I listened to my queen prattling about extra compost for her beloved radishes. That an almost useless vegetable merited better treatment than I did was, I knew, but a foreshadowing. Today's humiliation was nothing compared to what might happen if the cruel hand of despotism was allowed its full freedom. It was time a serf rose up and . . . grew a pair.

Plenty of space now that the peppers had their own plot . . . and one tomato looks much like another until it ripens. Mr. Stripey could be slipped in among Big Beef, or any of the others. She wouldn't be able to tell them apart. I pictured my wife pulling weeds right next to Mr. Stripey, never suspecting she was helping him grow strong. I'd be the one smiling then. Yes, let her suppose she reigned supreme until July's shimmering heat brought invading hordes of Mr. Stripey down upon the royal salad, sweeping all before them.

* * *

It turned cold overnight. I woke sometime before dawn under the faint translucence of snow through the sheer curtains. The garden was covered by the time we got up and I wish the memory of it was gone as well. My chief complaint with winter is the amount of time available for reflection, the long evenings I'll have to spend considering what happened.

She has forgiven me, yes, though it hasn't completely taken away the sting of defeat. There is suspicion, no . . . not suspicion . . . certainty, though I haven't any proof. I put Mr. Stripey's picture up on the refrigerator as a hint that I'm wise to her. It might have been a mistake, because now I have to see my innocent wife smiling whenever she opens the door. Otherwise, my darling has been magnanimous in victory, refusing to sully herself with recrimination after my apology. It only makes it worse.

I had come home from a business trip that last week of June. We went for an evening stroll around the garden to enjoy the lush greenery of success. I remember the broccoli was doing great, with large, well-formed heads. I was looking forward to it after several days of hotel food, also the carrots and peas that were just about ready for picking. There were lots of half-sized peppers that promised an abundant harvest. The tomatoes seemed to be thriving . . .

"What's that . . . "

"Hmm?" went my darling.

I wanted to scream, to accuse with thunderous voice.

I stepped between the vines to stare at a hole in the middle of the tomato bed. I had to get down on hands and knees for a closer inspection because I couldn't believe it. There wasn't so much as a root left. Plainly, any of the usual garden pests would have eaten the fruit and left the vine, but Mr Stripey had been eradicated entirely.

"Is something wrong, dear?"

Oh, how she must have enjoyed that. I couldn't answer because, scuttling crab-like back and forth over the ground in a frantic search for evidence, I was temporarily beyond speech. She might have dropped something, an incriminating work glove, or left a footprint. The faintest impression of her petite size sevens would have been enough! Pushing aside the draining sense of futility stealing over me, I leapt up to check the compost bin—a pathetic last hope. If she had been so foolish as to dump the bodies . . . but she had not been foolish.

"Some of our tomatoes are gone."

It was hard, very hard, to get that out with a level voice. I wanted to scream, to accuse with thunderous voice.

"Oh, what a shame," she said in a tone which approached disappointment, but never quite got there. "It must be those darn rabbits again."

Rabbits. Married twenty years and she was actually proposing rabbits. My dear Shelley, sharer of all my secret dreams, had looked at me with guileless eyes and tossed that off without effort. I felt like I needed to sit down. What was I to answer?

"I don't think it was rabbits." This was pointless, but some resistance had to be shown no matter how pitiful. Whatever dignity I had left demanded it.

"Well, maybe it was Zack," she offered.

The neighbor's creepy teenager—how clever. It was even faintly possible.

"Zack. Yeah."

"I'll have a word with Jada. We can't have him pulling up our veggies."

"Right."

My eyes swept over the bare spot. I was puzzling over how she'd known Mr. Stripey was planted there among the others. Maybe it was just that I'd grown too predictable, but in that scary moment it seemed like my wife knew my thoughts as soon as I did.

"Strange," I mused, looking deep into her eyes, "he went for the ones in the middle. All the others are fine."

My darling's gaze was as untroubled as her reply. "I see that. I'm feeling very irritated with Zack right now. Just wait 'til I see his mother."

And then she broke me:

"Do you remember which variety you planted there?"

I like the way that, in history books, generals are said to have retired from the field when they realized the battle was lost. It's a pleasant thought. The books do not describe them galloping away in terrible panic, or tearfully imploring their god to save them. No, they simply rode back to headquarters at a measured pace, maybe smoked a cigarette, drank a glass of wine, and then withdrew with dignity to wherever defeated generals retire. Not too bad a fate, but what I'm most interested in, and the books do not reveal, was their state of mind. Were they already planning their next battle?

I went for a walk through the fresh snow this morning. Past the garden, down the little slope that bottoms out on a raspberry bramble. Naked winter stems allowed me to see beyond what is in summer an impenetrably thorny thicket. There's a clearing in the midst of the bramble that is not even hinted at during the growing season. It's just the right size.

There will be no talk of sharing, next spring. After the soil warms, and the clearing is once again occluded by sharp green, Mr. Stripey will rise. In secret glade shall he grow strong, warded from the dread implements of royal disdain. Under mid-summer sky will obsession be rewarded, sweeter for the waiting. Mr. Stripey is my destiny. I can already taste it.

Name That Flower Part!
by Mae Fayne

Show your flower-power by matching the name to the flower part.

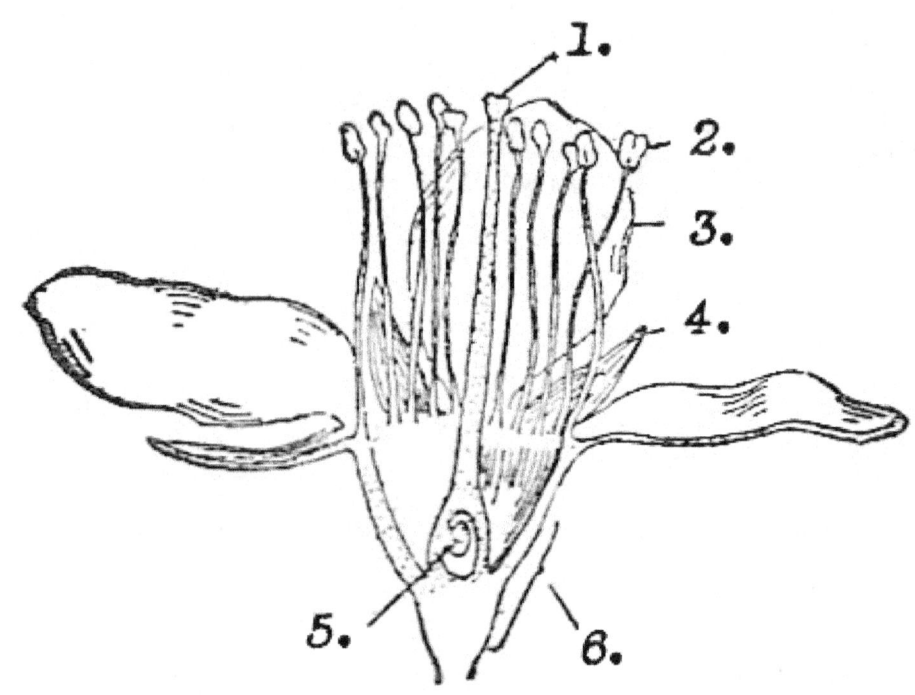

A. Ovule
B. Petal
C. Stamen
D. Receptacle
E. Sepal
F. Pistil

Illustration from *A Text-Book of Botany for Colleges*, 1917.

Answers:
A.5, B.3, C.2, D.6, E.4, F.1

Green Thumb

by Marian Kaplun Shapiro

You tried to teach me when
I was 33. You
were five. Just stick it back
in the dirt, you said, handing
me the prickly arm of
the one-inch cactus it
had broken off from. Kindly,
I explained about living
things: Birds. Animals.
People. Arms and blood vessels.
Plants, with their capillary
systems I was none too sure
of. Except for roots.
I knew about roots.
Just try, you insisted.
I did. We did.
It did. Many many
cacti later, they did.
Arm into dirt, arm
into dirt.

What made her so certain?
When we talk about it, I
at 68, she at 40,
mother of three, she still
hasn't got the slightest clue.
Nor do I. How roots
grow. How what seems dead
may come alive again. How
children know.

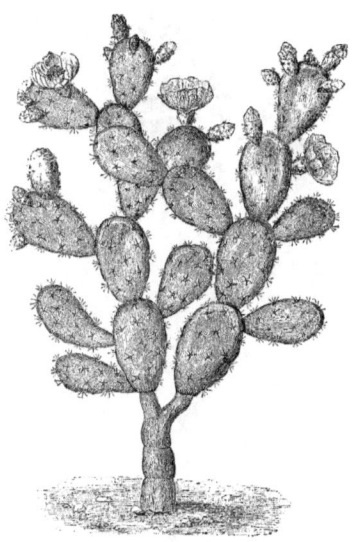

Oak and Ivy

by Cynthia Rosi

When the ivy seed first planted
in the warmth of spring's darkness
it whispered to the tree: "Let me.
I will nestle. I will entwine.
I will cradle you."
The curious tree
checked frequently
its roots' companion.
Will it tickle like insects?
Bring news like birds?
Aggravate like mold?
In a storm, the oak shuddered
at lightning's whine
at the branches crack.
Ivy danced up the trunk.
Oak waved
his leaves with ivy leaves
in concert, conducted
by wind.
In autumn when the trees
sang pink and gold
and flame
Ivy was companion yellow
or contrasting orange.
Together, they were a complementary pair.
"I will be with you until you die," Ivy
whispered, as her trunk thickened
and she gripped Oak with hairy fingers
that coursed over Oak's bark like
new veins.
Is it a choice, breathing
or companionship? Merry Ivy so thick
Oak's forgotten his own leaves. The birds'
chatter no longer clear,
the itch of insects
insisting, deep, and rotten.
Where does Ivy stop and I begin? Oak
wondered as his thoughts dimmed.
Oak and Ivy, forever
together.
Ivy and Oak.
Ivy.

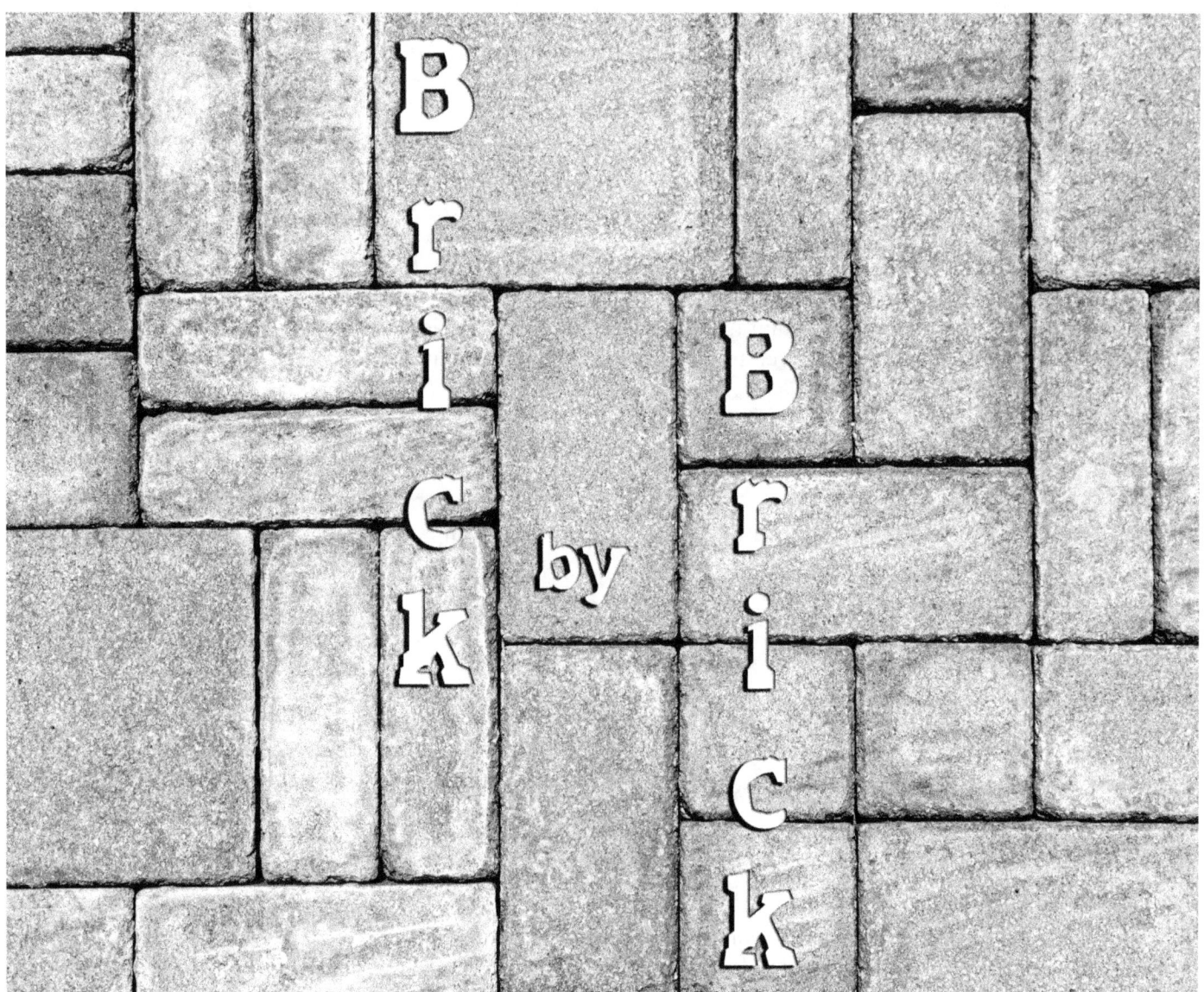

by Gayla Mills

Imagine a back yard full of blueberry bushes, plum trees, wild grass, and a profusion of flowers, with a curving brick walkway that carries you along a path half hidden from view. You arrive at a bench under a mature crepe myrtle, and you sit in its shade with book in hand, pink blossoms at your feet and the scent of jasmine in the air.

That's what I imagined after we'd settled into our new home, as I looked out over the barren back yard with the few remnants of weeds and scrub bushes that our dogs hadn't yet destroyed. Undaunted, I decided to bring my dreams to life, beginning with the walkway.

In the process, I learned everything there is to know about building such a path. If you come on the journey with me step by step, you, too, can create a garden wonder. Simply begin as follows:

1. Have an argument with your spouse about the placement of the walkway. You want one with some gentle curves that can be accented with plantings. He wants a direct path that will get him straight to his shed. He agrees to your plan if you're willing to do the work. This seems like a good idea at the time.

2. Go to the masonry store to choose from among dozens of brick pavers. Bring a sample brick from your patio so you can confirm that nothing in the storeroom will match.

3. Lay down newspaper in the shape and direction you want the walk to take, then use whatever leftover spray paint you have in the basement to mark the grass edges, imagining this to be Martha Stewart style. Now you know where to dig. Note that the neighbors are looking from their second story windows at your newspaper walk trimmed with silver and blue paint and concluding that it's time to move.

4. Start digging with a spade. Realize after two feet that you have forty-eight to go.

5. Look at the piles you've created after removing the grass, the middle layer of topsoil, and the bottom layer of clay. Conclude that these piles will soon turn into mountains if you don't develop a strategy.

This is called stonework, and usually you pay people with experience and tools to do this type of thing.

6. Ask Husband for advice. He helpfully suggests making several much-needed garden beds with the half-hidden rock from around the yard. He notes that all you'll need to do is move the topsoil after assembling the rocks. He returns to his sandwich.

7. Spend several hours excavating stones with a rock bar and moving them across the yard. These will need to be individually selected and chiseled so that they interlock, creating a stable foot-high border that can hold the soil in place. This is called stonework, and usually you pay people with experience and tools to do this type of thing. This is why normal people go to Lowe's and buy premade stacking borders.

8. Take time to admire what you have accomplished so far. You have now cleared five feet of walkway. Several large mounds of discarded grass and clay litter the yard. The dogs have been practicing their digging skills by expanding the holes where the rocks once rested peacefully. You now have the beginnings of a garden bed large enough for two tomato plants and some basil.

9. Watch the truck arrive prematurely to deliver the brick and sand. It takes a special forklift to move the heavy loads to your front lawn, where they are crushing the only grass you have left. The sun is at high noon in late July, too hot to work. Time for a nap.

10. Observe that it's day three and the first garden bed is finally ready for the soil. Clear ten more feet of walkway, sorting the material as you dig into new piles: topsoil for the beds, grass clumps for the compost, clay for the holes, and silver painted scrub for the trash. You've made excellent progress. Don't look at the untouched sand and massive brick cube on your way to the car.

11. On day four you should continue throwing the soggy tennis ball to your OCD dog every ten seconds while you work, because otherwise she'll lay a guilt trip on you. Try to ignore the other dog, who's been napping on top of your piles, then tracking the soil back into the house through the dog door when the mood strikes. Stop thinking about the moral aspects of euthanizing animals in their prime.

12. Recall that it's Saturday, the day of the Farmer's Market. They are selling lots of heirloom plants. It would be nice to have something to put in those new garden beds. Spend some time shopping for plants instead of digging.

13. Speculate that these plants will need something better than that old topsoil crap. You'd best find your digging shovel and get some of that lovely compost you've been nursing since last fall. Coax it through the bottom door of the composting barrel. As sweat drips into your new wheelbarrow, don't think about returning to the air conditioned house.

14. After planting, watering, and admiring the first new bed, measure out the next ten feet of walk, which accomplishes nothing but is easy to do. Notice that your right shoulder isn't working quite the way it used to.

15. Observe that you've spent two more days of heavy digging, and you're almost done removing the soil— only eight feet left. Don't think about the *plantar fasciitis* irritated by the spade work that is causing constant pain to the bottom of your right foot. It will go away if you stop standing or walking for a few weeks.

16. Shovel sand into the wheelbarrow, then after you've dumped a couple of loads onto the pathway, screed it with a scrap 2-by-4. Curse the dog as he lies down in your carefully leveled sand. And then does it again.

> Don't think about the *plantar fasciitis* irritated by the spade work that is causing constant pain to the bottom of your right foot.

17. Get a couple dozen bricks from the front yard (from the cube of five hundred) and begin laying the herringbone pattern that will curve from the house to the shed. After discovering that your tile saw won't cut this brick, realize that you'll need to rent a paver saw to make all those angled cuts on the edges. Get on the Internet to check prices. This is a good time to play some Spider Solitaire.

18. Curse the day you chose a lovely herringbone with a curve rather than the straight walk with an easy running pattern and no cuts that your husband suggested.

19. Count up all the calories you burned this week, just for the hell of it. Reflect on the shortness of life. Don't wonder what the neighbors are thinking about the four hundred and eighty-eight bricks and one ton pile of sand still on the front lawn.

20. Now go take a nap. ❇

Penstemon
by Judith Offer

Plant penstemon
If you want exuberance,
In pinks and purples
And rosey protuberance.

©123RF Stock Photo/Tamara Kulikova

Cows With Names Make 3.4 Percent More Milk

by Bruce Holland Rogers

Art by Janae Lehto

When Brenda was still a teenager she liked to quote those findings to visitors. Most everyone under-stood that it wasn't really the names that made for better production, but visitors would still chuckle appreciatively when Brenda reeled them off. "That's Mandy Pie with the black circle around her eye, and the one next to her is Foxy for her favorite forage. She'll walk through an acre of alfalfa to get to meadow foxtail. Over by the fence is Honey Lemon. You never know which mood you're going to get from her, the sweet or the sour." Brenda could go on to name any cow within sight. She did her share of work with them every day, after all.

In college she was a dairy science major, even though her father had told her, "Sweet Pie, you'd just be taking over my debts." She had plans for improving the farm. She could supply restaurants with butter and fresh cheeses unlike anything they could get elsewhere. The farm might need a new name.

The first boys Brenda met at school didn't impress her. Like most of the girls in her dorm, she hooked up with guys at parties, but nothing ever came of a night of making out. If she saw those guys again at all, they often didn't remember her name. One morning, Brenda's roommate was happy because the boy she'd had sex with the night before had asked for her phone number. Brenda said, "Do you even hear what you're saying?" Right then and there, Brenda was finished with hooking up. She wasn't going to meet the right guy at school.

Her senior year, in the second week of the term, she was waiting in the hallway before Introduction to Finance. "So," said a guy who was waiting next to her, "you're a finance major?" Brenda shook her head, told him she was majoring in dairy science. "Dairy science?" he said. He had blue eyes. Nice eyes, though now his gaze was flitting back and forth between meeting hers and looking anywhere else. She could tell he was struggling to find the next thing to say. He settled on repeating, "Dairy science." Then, "As in cows, huh?" Finally, he held out his hand. "Colin," he said. "Colin Downs. Colin Tristan Downs." He smiled.

It wasn't a bad start, but what sealed the deal, over the course of the semester, dinners out, movies, a picnic, and eventually a trip home to meet her parents, were the nicknames that he rained down on her in a succession that promised never to end:

"Ladybug"
"Spark Plug"
"Mama Moo"
"Marmalady"
"Miss Butter"
"Mighty Smacky High Holy Bee-atchy"
"Brenda Pooks"
"Applesauce"
"Sugar Twitch"
"Angel"

"Killer Bee"

"Poptart"

Five years later, they were running Summer Peach Creamery together, and although Colin commuted to a job in town and had no hand in managing the herd, he certainly knew Cowzilla from Betty Boop. ❁

"In the Produce Aisle"

A Vegetable Soap Opera by Mae Fayne & Angus Skillet

Starring:

Tommy Tomato

Lucy Lettuce

Patrick Potato

Tommy and Lucy are in love!

The diabolical Patrick butts in. . .

Tommy mashes Patrick!

"My hero!" (THE END)

Le Cactus, Antique Postcard, *Greenwoman* Collection

Don't let this happen to *your* business!

Arnie: There goes the 5th customer today that asked for *Greenwoman*.

Fred: And she looked pretty darn mad when you said we didn't carry it.

Arnie: We'd better get in here, quick.

Fred: Hells, yes! We want to keep the ladies happy!

Women love *Greenwoman*.
Keep them happy—place your business order today!

Growing Locally

A Morning in the Garden
by Larry Stebbins

A journal entry from June 9, 2008:

As I sit on a bench near my vegetable garden and drink in the morning air I am reminded why I love to garden. It is 6:30 in the morning and the dappled morning sun is just starting to peek through my neighbor's hedge. The warmth of the sunlight is overcoming the moist dawn air. Dew, nature's washcloth, has settled on the leaves of my frilly lettuces and wrinkly spinach. The onions have sprouted and point to the heavens like so many daggers. And who would suspect that the tiny filigreed leaves of the carrots would soon sport a bulbous root of such splendor.

In one corner of my garden is my tomato patch. They are just starting to flower. This is an unusual flower and plant. I know from my botany training that most all plants in the tomato family are all or part poisonous. Many like deadly nightshade, jimsonweed and tobacco do harm to our bodies. And I can't forget the hot peppers that burn our mouths and throats. Their five-pointed flowers don't point toward the sun like most but instead pay homage to the darkness of the earth, as if to hint at their inner character.

There are many other five-petaled flowers in my garden. The delicate alpine strawberries, raspberries, cherry, plum and apple trees all are in bloom. They belong to the rose family. So many delicious fruits come from this lineage. Their flowers point skyward, and to the best of my knowledge none are poisonous. Hmmm, I can only wonder what all this means.

Under a nearby Ponderosa pine is a small patch of mushrooms. They are ominously white. Grown in the damp twilight they seem like ghostly imitations of their sun-borne cousins, the flowers. The caps of these fungi are like over-turned blossoms. Again, like the tomato family pointing downward to the depths of the planet below. I marvel at the interplay of light and darkness and how it seems to be a dance that only nature understands.

A few honeybees are starting to circle and land on a rather sprawling patch of oregano in full bloom. They wiggle and prod their way through what to them must be a jungle of leaves and stems. Finding that nectar rich source they linger and extend their long proboscis for a drink. I know somewhere, as if by magic, they will transform this sweet syrup into the ambrosia of honey. How different are the wasps that are landing on the ground to sip from a small puddle of muddy water. I can see one that is flying under my deck to use this slurry to build a nest out of paper and mud. No honey there. Under my feet there is a small squadron of black ants. Moving in what seems like a purposeful march to the hinterlands. They live deep in the soil, under all the activity from above.

Once more I see the relationship of the honeybee, flower, sun, and honey. It is contrasted to the wasp of the interzone of the sun and earth then to the ants of the recesses of the soil.

The yellow and orange daisy-like flowers of calendula have attracted some Admiral butterflies. What an amazing partnership. I look at the flowers and sense they are butterflies that are tethered to the earth. If only they could break away from their bondage they would be as free as the butterflies that frequent them. As I sit there overlooking my future bounty I catch a slight waft of lavender. It is unmistakable. The perfume of the flower does what the flowers are unable to do. Although the flowers cannot be liberated from their stems the blossoms fly into the cosmos on the wings of the fragrance. Even the delicate petals fade and disappear after time. In their place is a seed, a promise of what will be.

My friends ask me if I hear God speak to me in the garden. I believe we all can hear Him, but we must listen with all our senses. ❁

Gates of Perception:
An Interview with Jane Gates

"I find it fascinating that whatever happens in my life always forms a stepping stone for something that crops up in the future."

Greenwoman: Jane, I have to ask, how does it feel to be a polymath? You hold an advanced degree in art and design (Rhode Island School of Design) and made a living in Europe as an artist and lyricist. You've worked in the green industry for 25 years doing everything from running nurseries to designing gardens and were into eco-conscious designs before it was hip. You've worked in what I think of as "regular" business as well, creating seminars for training programs in the industrial and health care sectors. You're a licensed contractor in California, you write extensively for several California and national publications, you create your own instructional videos, you design and sell T-shirts and scarves, you have a new book out and you are doing some gorgeous designs for seed packets. The last time we talked, you commented that you "do everything but eat, sleep and make money." (That cracked me up.) And then you said, to illustrate, that you were getting ready to rebuild some bathroom built-in cabinets!

My first question is how did those cabinets turn out? I'm kidding, but really—how do you do all the things you do?

Jane Gates: [Laughs.] The cabinets turned out just fine. Now I'm working on replacing the innards of my irrigation valves—and I hate plumbing!

I have led a colorful life but, bottom line, I suppose I am a genuine "earth mother." I'm lucky to be gifted with both artistic and practical skills that I want to use to help people reconnect with the joy of being part of something bigger. I've always felt anything we do is just an expression of who we are and I've played with using that expression through a lot of different job media.

Greenwoman: How does this expression fit in with your latest big endeavor, your new book *All the Garden's a Stage*?

Jane Gates: The book, in a way, puts a lot of these pieces together. When I was young I worked in theater (mostly designing stage sets for school and summer stock theater). I always loved plants and living organically, and between the art, the writing, the music, or working in nurseries I would somehow get the bills paid.

The book compares putting together a theatrical production with creating a garden: cast your characters (plants like "water mavens," "mountaineers," "tribes of the prairies," or "beach babes") for the right roles; build in systems to support and show off your show (lighting, irrigation/drainage, natural pest control); and design sets (hardscapes: pathways, structures, water features, recycled materials, etc.) that will help your plant performers bring your script to life. I love gardening. Most of it is fun. And there are so many excellent tomes on the market on gardening and landscaping. Most of which are full of brilliant information but aren't fun at all! I wanted to make learning about gardening as much fun as doing it.

Greenwoman: Can you tell us a little about the process of putting the book together?

Jane Gates: I put a year and a half of intensive work (7 days/week, 10 hours/day) into writing it. Actually, maybe one quarter of the time went into writing the book. The rest went into learning about writing, formatting, editing (painful for someone who talks as much as I do!) and photography. The last was a genuine project for someone who always cut heads off my photos of people. Fortunately, I was confined to plants and people escaped beheading. I also used so many of my Facebook friends to fill in photos from other parts of the country. And I had wonderful support from my local friends who kept me laughing, proofread, taught me about photography, and supplied feedback all along the intensive journey. I worried I would make mistakes and felt insecure that I didn't know everything. Then I realized no one knows everything and I will just have to forgive myself if I make those inevitable mistakes.

Happy performers in a well-staged garden—Gates' style.

So there it is; the story of *All the Garden's a Stage*. I lived an amazingly frugal life for that year—no heat, no air-conditioning, no meals out, no entertainment. Didn't have time for any of that anyway. Just went out and harvested whatever matured in my vegetable garden, ran with my dogs to stay exercised, and repaired whatever needed fixing by myself. I hope someone out there enjoys reading it!

Greenwoman: You told me that this book came during a very challenging point in your life.

Jane Gates: When the housing recession hit, I was living here in the "fastest growing city in California" [Los Angeles] so my busy designing business screeched to a halt. My gallery of 18 years folded. I looked in the mirror and realized I was no longer young and this was the best I would ever look or feel. I watched my mother degenerate from a beautiful, high-functioning woman into a fearful zombie with Alzheimer's disease. And I suddenly realized I was flirting with depression for the first time in my life. Thus the book was born. If I couldn't earn a living, I at least had to feel productive and useful. So I took all those things of the past and rolled them into a pastry dough to bake up yet another attempt to remind the world (and myself) that we are all part of a bigger, more awesome presentation —not just a bunch of detached money-grubbers scratching to be more important than the next guy.

Greenwoman: I read your beautiful post, "Why do Artists Paint?" on your website earlier this year. You start off by talking about the artist's deep need to express his or herself and the comfort that comes in doing what you're "made to do," even in a society that does not appreciate the arts as it should. There's a wonderful section about your lifelong connection with nature and I'd like to end with these words:

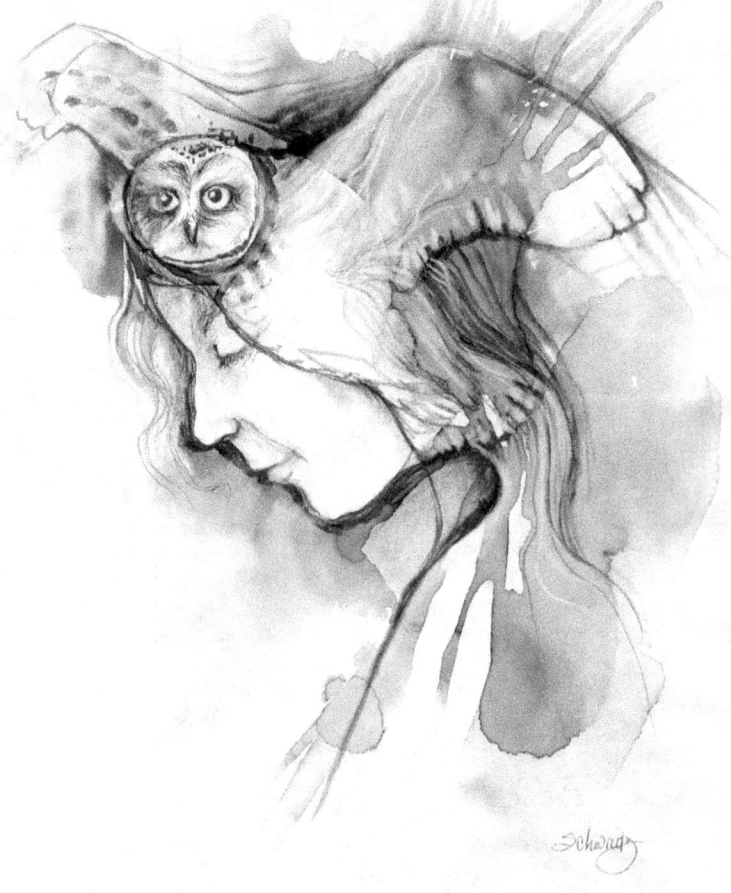

"I paint because I love doing it and because I am on a mission. I want to express the joy that comes of filling life with the appreciation of this magnificent planet and the graceful, interdependent dance of life that populates this earth. I hope that joy will infect others through my work. All artists have their own personal reasons to paint. I think most of us hope our work will not only be appreciated, but have some helpful impact on those who view it. Well, at least that's why I paint." ✽

You can find Jane Gates online listed under "The Garden Coach Directory," at her gardening blog, GardenGates, or her art website, "Jane Schwartz Gates, artist," where you can see her paintings, illustrations, cartoons, and pet portraits.

"Feminine Wisdom" by Jane Gates

Buckley's
HOMESTEAD SUPPLY

- Beekeeping supplies

- Soap making supplies

- Cheese and yogurt making supplies

- Organic feed for goats, rabbits and chickens

- Canning and fermenting supplies

- And much, much more!

(719) 358-8510 • 1501 W. Colorado Ave., Colorado Springs, CO
www.buckleyshomesteadsupply.com

Almost Too Happy
by
Simone Martel

This time, my mother says it, as we step outside onto the deck overlooking my garden, but my father might as well have.

"That climbing rose is happy." She nods toward the peach-flowering tangle atop the arbor. "Almost too happy."

Admittedly, a few thorny canes have flung themselves into the nearby star magnolia tree. But "almost too happy" in my parents' language means too much. I feel judged.

Other plants-gone-wild in my garden include the nasturtiums trailing out of my potted lemon tree and romping across the driveway, and a stand of pink hollyhocks growing higher than the roof and prone to keeling over in a wind.

My parents' garden, by contrast, is a picture of monochromatic order and restraint. Black mondo grass edges gravel paths. Clumps of sculptural succulents punctuate borders of neat ground cover.

It wasn't always so. I remember, as a child, peering up into the faces of orange and yellow dahlias the size of my head and galloping past banks of purple bearded iris and gold tiger lilies—memories tinted with the saturated colors of old home movies.

My parents say their tastes are simpler now. They've gotten rid of many plants or replaced them with less demanding ones. Partly, this editing is a result of age. They no longer grow bearded iris or other perennials that need dividing, because my father, the digger-upper, has rebelled. Partly, though, the change is aesthetic. My father may refuse to wrestle with clumps of agapanthus, but he's happy to spend an afternoon with his electric hedge clippers carving camellias into gumdrops and lollipops.

My garden seems to bother my parents more than it used to, its messiness more apparent to them, its beauty less so.

As they drive away, I wave goodbye from the front yard where aloe, spider plants, fuchsias, plumbago, abutilon, ferns, Japanese anemone, and roses jostle each other. A few years ago, my husband built a fence to contain the abundance. Low and slatted, it's vaguely California craftsman style, to match our house. On rainy days when I sit reading on the living room sofa, feeling stir-crazy, the slats look like prison bars. They seem to separate me from the rest of the world, to hold me in.

The fence can't hold my garden in, though. The ferns lean through the bars and the 'Cecile Brunner' rose reaches over the top railing, trailing thorny fingers across the clumps of hen-and-chicks that bulge over the sidewalk.

> **Maybe the flamboyant, almost-out-of-control garden that surrounds our house reflects the family that lives inside of it.**

After my parents' car turns the corner, I walk down the driveway to the backyard again, past the raised vegetable bed I've built to catch the heat reflected from the cement driveway and the south-facing wall of the house. Here, peppers, tomatoes, and cucumbers do as well as they can in the foggy Bay Area. Springtime lettuces have bolted and flowered, attracting beneficial insects. Woolly pink yarrow has grown out of the cracked cement. I let it stay.

In general, I welcome volunteer plants to pop up where they will. Today, though, perhaps because of my mother's comment about the rose, the bronze fennel growing in the strip of earth alongside the driveway and listing into my path bothers me. I kick it aside. Then I fetch clippers and cut it down. When I lug the ferny, anise-scented stalks to the compost pile, however, I discover a fat yellow and black caterpillar clinging to a frond and I regret my temporary urge to tidy. This lushness supports life.

I sit on the wooden stairs leading down from the deck to the lawn. Beside me, the pink hollyhocks sway to and fro in the breeze.

"Some twine would solve that," my mother has suggested, but since the stalks are more-or-less vertical, I've had no desire to lash them together like pirates' victims about to walk the plank. Besides, I don't own twine.

Irritation flares up in me. I like the hollyhocks, the peach roses on the arbor. They make me happy.

And why is "happy" my parents' code for wild?

And what's wrong with wild?

Maybe the flamboyant, almost-out-of-control garden that surrounds our house reflects the family that lives inside of it. Doors have been slammed in there, plastic water bottles (empty) have been thrown, voices have been raised. We get a little crazy. Appropriate, then, that when my son dyed his hair for Crazy Hair Day, his dad photographed him outside, in front of a princess tree with flowers the exact same shade of purple.

Crazy Hair Day was in elementary school, though. Lately, the craziness has been less fun, more painful. My parents would be surprised, possibly shocked, at what goes on in there some nights. I certainly never called my mother a bitch—but then she never unplugged the modem and disconnected me from my video game at bedtime. Life before computers was easier on parents, I suspect.

Beside me, the hollyhocks careen in the rising wind. Maybe I should buy that twine. Maybe my garden, my life, could use more discipline and order.

This is being middle aged: pissing off my son, pissed at my parents. I feel old and immature, at once. I'm a mom, weighing my words because the most innocent comment is sure to offend, and I'm a daughter rolling my eyes behind my parents' backs.

Physically, too, I'm neither young nor old. Or perhaps I'm both, depending on which parts of me I focus on. Mostly I'm good at ignoring the wrinkly bits, just as I hardly notice that the hollyhocks' leathery leaves that rustle near my shoulder are speckled with rust and riddled with tiny insect holes. Why worry about that, when, overhead, pink flowers are pasted against a pale blue sky, the colors lifted from a Japanese print?

Soon enough, I'll be old. Maybe then I'll chop down these hollyhocks, or their descendants, annoyed by their constant movement, irritated by their imperfections. For now, I'll choose to focus on their beauty. For just a little longer, I'll raise my chin, follow the swaying stalks twelve, fifteen feet up, until I see nothing but those pink disks glowing against a cloudless sky. ✳

Veggie Tug o' War
(An old embroidery transfer pattern revisited.)
Mae Payne & Angus Skillet

HENDERSON'S
GIANT IMPERIAL JAPANESE
MORNING GLORIES

EMPEROR OF JAPAN SEE No 1 PKT 15¢
EMPRESS OF JAPAN   „ 2 „ 15¢
COUNT ITO   „ 3 „ 15¢
YAMAGATA   „ 4 „ 15¢
MIXED ABOVE 4 AND OTHER VARIETIES .. 15¢
RUFFLED & FRILLED MIXED SEE No 5 „ 25¢
DOUBLE FLOWERING MIXED Nos 6,7,8
      AND OTHER VARIETIES „ 25¢
THE COLLECTION OF THE
ABOVE SEVEN PACKETS
$ 1.00
FREE BY MAIL

Sadie & Ruby ♥ Greenwoman Magazine

Sadie: My mind's still reeling from the thought-provoking articles and stories I read last night.

Ruby: Mine too! *Greenwoman*'s a great mind trip.

Sadie: Can't wait for the next volume. . .

Ruby: Neither can I.

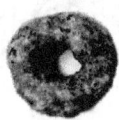  

THE NEW VICTORY GARDEN

By LaManda Joy

Illustration by Joe Wirtheim

Learning from the past to create a brighter future—what could be smarter? It's something we're hooked into now more than ever: rebuilding community, growing and cooking our own wholesome food (or buying it locally)—activities and values that harken to our not-so-distant past. As historian and author LaManda Joy shows us, Victory Gardens were originally about wartme shortages, but their valuable lessons can bolster a victorious "We Can Do It!" attitude today.—*Editor*

Over the last 70 years, the second World War's (WWII) Victory Garden movement has gathered a patina of quaintness. What was a massive and historic effort has been reduced to a few sound-bites about "20 million gardens" and "40% of the nation's produce was home grown."

Recently, however, the story has crept out of the collective shadows to become a tale that can reinvigorate today's families and communities. In 2009, when I started studying Chicago Victory Gardens, I encountered, on the wall at our local butcher's, a photo of a World War II Victory Garden not far from my house.
I was intrigued by the orderliness, the giant "V" for Victory, and the American flag proudly flying. It made me think of my family's WWII stories and my own love of food gardening that I had been chronicling in my blog (http://www.theyarden.com). As an armchair historian, the idea seized me that perhaps we could really learn something from this important story.

When I first set out to uncover exactly how a city teaches its citizenry to grow their own food, I had to overcome some biases. Namely, I assumed that more people came from agrarian backgrounds and therefore the WWII effort was a no-brainer—surely Chicagoan's could grow their own food, they merely chose not to since the urban environment offered what they needed.

What I learned surprised me. As far back as 1908 the famous landscape designer Jens Jensen was designing Chicago parks with allotment gardens because he was concerned that urban children didn't understand where their food came from. This led to the uncovering of an astonishing statistic—90% of Chicago Victory Gardeners had never gardened before at all.

Biases firmly shaken, I sat back and pondered the effort and dedication of the people in charge of organizing the Victory Garden movement. How daunting it must have been to understand that if Chicago didn't grow its own food, shortages would have a debilitating impact on the city's well being. Thankfully those brave planners in 1942 were unified in their effort to win the war.

Before I get too carried away with Victory Gardens in general, it's important to remember that WWII ultimately claimed 60 million casualties worldwide—40 million of whom were civilians. Most of the world's nations were involved in the conflict and the major players put their full economic, industrial and scientific capacity toward winning—to the point that the lines between civilian and military were blurred. U.S. forces were deployed to 50 fronts at the height of the war and the Quartermaster General was responsible for providing 24 million meals per day. Homegrown produce was not a luxury—it was a necessity. Food was one of the many elements that were in short supply. Fabric was rationed to the point that collars and hemlines got shorter to pre-

"... 90% of Chicago Victory Gardeners [during World War II] had never gardened before at all."

serve resources. Women's nylons were a rarity. Metal scraps and cooking fat were collected to reuse for military manufacturing. A popular saying of the day was:

> Eat it up.
> Wear it out.
> Make it do.
> Do without.

To every American wondering where their next meal might be coming from there was no question what the "Victory" in Victory Garden stood for.

In the spring of 1942 all that was on the minds of civic leaders was the impending need of almost 3.5 million Chicago citizens. Many people remembered WWI where a similar "War Garden" effort was employed to mixed success. In the words of one of the Chicago Victory Garden leaders, George Donaghue:

> "Victory gardening in WWII was radically different in character and extent from the corresponding activity in WWI. Lack of sustained promotion, absence of any organized scheme of promoting gardening and generally haphazard and wasteful methods

destroyed much of the usefulness and productivity of the so-called war garden movement in WWI.

In WWII, at least in Chicago, most of these faults were recognized before actual fighting took place. A thorough and complete scheme of organization was set up. Largely due to the aid of the Chicago Park District and the local office of Civilian Defense there was a continuous program of promotion, stimulation, guidance and active help."

This "thorough and complete scheme of organization" used every media outlet available at the time. Compared to our media-saturated world, radio and newspaper articles don't seem like much, but through using these simple tools (customized gardening instruction provided by local newspapers and lectures) success was achieved. One local radio station had a daily program called "Know Your Onions!" that ran daily and helped gardeners with timely issues such as pests or watering suggestions.

By 1943, the Chicago Victory Garden effort had really taken off. Here are some amazing facts:

• 14,000 plots were gardened by children on Chicago Park District land (30,000 plots were set aside, but the spring of 1943 was so miserable weather-wise more than half the kids—and probably their parents—gave up.)

• The largest Victory Garden in the United States was in Chicago's North Park neighborhood. Eight hundred families farmed this gigantic garden.

• Chicago-based companies such as Marshall Fields and International Harvester donated seeds and garden equipment.

• A city ordinance prevented theft from Victory Gardens with fines of $600-$2,400 in today's currency.

• An estimated 172,000 home Victory Gardens sprang up in 1943 alone.

• Private property/city lots or park property housed 908 acres of community gardens.

• Communities held dozens of "harvest festivals" in the fall of 1943 including a city-wide festival at Soldier Field attended by thousands.

The old koan "no matter how things change they stay the same" is fitting when you think of gardening today versus gardening in WWII or gardening 10,000 years ago at the dawn of civilization. The basic elements remain the same: sunlight, healthy soil, water, seeds. The planners of the Chicago Victory Garden movement cleverly crafted educational materials around the basics of food growing and made them specific to the Chicago climate. They are almost as relevant today as they were then.

However, one element that is unique to that time is a strong emphasis on crops' nutritional value. This underscores that gardening wasn't for leisure—it was for creating a healthy war machine.

Ironically, during the Great Depression there was a lot of food but no money to buy it. This situation flipped in WWII where there was more money but little food. When it came time to draft soldiers for WWII, 30% of potential recruits were malnourished to the point where they couldn't join the military. Military-based industry was quickly raising wages and women were entering the workforce for the first time. ("Daycare" was one of the innovations of WWII.) All these workers and soldiers needed to be fit in order to perform their essential tasks. All food-related education, especially education related to gardening, focused on the nutritional value of food as well as balancing shortages with available supplies (for example, cottage cheese became popular in WWII as a meat substitute).

Another often-overlooked aspect of the Victory Garden movement is food preservation. In short-season climates such as Chicago, methods of food preservation were essential. Traditional hot-bath canning was the primary method of food preservation, although brining, dehydrating, and other methods were encouraged. In fact, the manufacturing of pressure cookers was considered so important that the government diverted materials that could have been used for munitions to their creation and oversaw their distribution. It is estimated that five billion pints of food were preserved by home canners each summer of the war.

Growing up I heard a lot about WWII from my

To every American wondering where their next meal might be coming from there was no question what the "Victory" in Victory Garden stood for.

Greatest Generation parents. They met in 1941 and married before my dad was deployed to the occupation forces in Japan in 1945. On her 16th birthday, the first thing my mother did was go to the local munitions plant and get a job as a Rosie the Riveter. I had heard many, many WWII stories so I fully understood the "book-ends" of the war—-the bombing of Pearl Harbor in 1941 and V-J (Victory over Japan) Day in August of 1945. But the consequences of the war and the trajectory of Victory Gardens didn't end in the summer of 1945.

Left with the aftermath of this terrible conflict, the U. S. was occupied for many years patrolling, rebuilding, and cleaning up in its former "war theatres." The Cold War and the threat of communism were creeping into the American psyche, and for a while gardens continued to play a leading role. One poster proclaimed that growing a "Freedom Garden" helped with the post-war effort as "Food Fights the Red Menace." Fast forward a few years (to the late 1940's) and GIs began returning home for good to restart their lives. To help fight the new inflation, "Thrift Gardens" were encouraged to help keep food bills low.

Around the mid-1950's the food garden fell out of vogue and ornamental gardening became popular as all the women who had previously been working now had babies to care for and homes to beautify. Landscape gardening became a new way to keep up with the Joneses as TV dinners and other processed foods freed up time in the kitchen. Vegetable gardening, for most, was a distant memory associated with tough times and sadness.

The consequences of the war changed society and put us on the footing for the modern world in which we live. After the war, the industrial military complex reconfigured itself for peacetime industry and the post-war baby boom gave the country a population that called for drastically changed food systems. We are now living with the consequences of a mechanized food system directly related to WWII. It is ironic that agriculture—the skill that brought us civilization—has changed so radically.

Now we look back at the gardens of WWII as inspiration for a new, smaller, locally-based food system.

* * *

My research on Victory Gardens, which began in 2009, prompted me to try to prove Fredrick Hagel's quote, "We learn from history that we do not learn from history" wrong. The photo hanging on the wall at the neighborhood butcher's, showing a huge, productive Victory garden is what led to the birth of The Peterson Garden Project.

The Victory Garden in the photo didn't fit what that neighborhood lot looked like in 2009. Situated on private land, part of it was enclosed with a weedy chain-link fence with broken bottles and trash strewn inside. I stopped one day and stared at it long and hard to image what it had once been and, maybe, what it could become again.

After talking to our local alderman about the idea of reviving a Victory Garden we set to work telling people about the project. I thought that if 20 people wanted to participate it would be cool. That first summer our garden at Peterson and Campbell became the largest edible, organic garden in the city.

I call it The Peterson Garden Project because the story a passerby can't see is that we used the original WWII Victory Garden model to set up and manage the garden. I became the block captain—my duties were to recruit and manage the volunteers, provide direction, and keep morale high. (Yes, there were a few sing-a-longs.) There's a saying "strangers are the stuff friends are made of," and I learned that really fast with this project. People were intrigued by the story, the methods we were employing, and the fact that they were reliving history, and they came out of the woodwork to lend their

Groundwork for Victory

GROW MORE IN '44

skills, encouragement, and labor. A core volunteer team quickly formed (thank goodness) to help with the ever-growing garden community. Oh, and we had to teach over 50% of our gardeners and volunteers (approximately 400 people each summer) how to grow their own food. Some things never change . . .

The Peterson Garden Project provided victory for a lot of people—myself included. One man told our alderman that in 2009 he hadn't left his house all summer and in 2010 he was at the garden every day. One woman, so debilitated with grief over the Gulf oil spill, could only bring herself to get out of bed to tend her plot. (She recovered over the summer.) There are dozens of stories how a formerly weedy patch of ground with a humble yet illustrious past, reinvigorated a neighborhood and, some may say, a city.

My mother says I have more spunk than sense. This is true. But, in the case of The Peterson Garden Project, it worked out okay, and, as I said, it changed my life. 2012 is the 70th anniversary of WWII and I'm dedicating the year to honor the Victory Garden story by

mobilizing our gardeners, friends, and volunteers to put in five more large "Pop-up" Victory Gardens on Chicago's north side. We anticipate gardening with 2,000+ people. A huge percentage, no doubt, will need to be taught what a seed is, how it marries with the earth, and how, with a little love, water, and sunshine, seeds can create a million small Victories that touch us all.

Much has transpired in the 70 years since the first Victory Garden season of WWII. Again we are faced with fears about our food supply. Unlike WWII, however, our Victory is not collective but individual in nature. People are growing food to save money, learn a valuable skill, spend time outdoors, teach their children where food comes from, decrease their carbon footprint, and reconnect with their neighbors. These are new challenges for a new generation, and I hope that, with the efforts of a lot of neighbors, volunteers and friends, we can revive this great Victory Garden effort to create a new and lasting greatest—and greenest—generation.

Garden Haiku
by Patricia K. Nolan

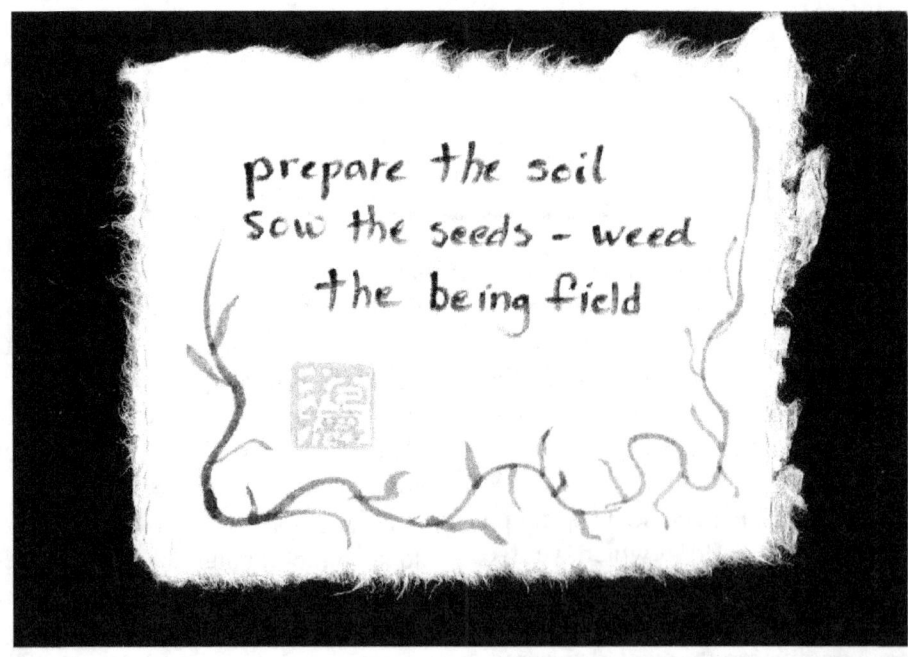

prepare the soil
sow the seeds - weed
the being field

Don't Fence Me In

Annette Hayden

© Can Stock Photo/bobloblaw66

Never Surrender!
by Tom Preble

Broken glass was everywhere around the hen house, but worse than broken glass was her shattered spirit. Just that morning we'd been relaxing in adirondak chairs, taking tea in the garden and admiring the fresh, perfect growth of our vegetables. "Why, we could be in *Mother Earth News* with these healthy vegetables," she'd told me. "Just look at the broccoli, cauliflower and squashes! For sure, this will be our first year of growing all of our own vegetables. The root cellar will be full!"

On that morning I couldn't help but agree. Garden leaves shone in the morning sun like sheet emeralds, the golden early light reflecting and passing through them. The leave's red and white veining stood out perfectly, ready for any magazine photo shoot. It was early June and our gardens were coming on in earnest. Warm days and rich soil were working their magic. To her, gardens are more than fresh, healthy food. The gardens nourish her spirit through a boundless optimism inherently found in growing life.

We'd left the plants to their exuberant growing and spent our day away from our eastern ranch, in town. That's when it happened. The warnings we heard on the radio said it was tracking east, across the northern part of the county. Our part of the county. Like a drunkard, a large, mature thunderstorm staggered north east, releasing its heavy burden of hail from forty thousand feet up.

Downward plummeted the heavy stones, an inch across. Downward, picking up speed, creating an icy down draft and sucking in ever more heavy stones behind them. A crushing load of hail, a storm of utter devastation staggered aimlessly eastward across high rolling prairie, pounding, relentlessly pummeling everything below. Cattle with nowhere to run bellowed in pain and terror in their pastures. Our chickens had retreated to the relative safety of their hen house, but not even vertical glass was safe from diamond-hard one-inch stones. Down they came, faster, faster until large stones lay four inches deep on the ground, completely covering the

42   Volume 3 • greenwomanmagazine.com

debris of their destruction. Trees were stripped of nearly all of their leaves, only fully out just the week before. Later whole limbs would die, the bark beaten off of them. Our chimney cap lay in the yard among drifts of shredded green leaves from the trees and vines. The sumptuous gardens of that morning didn't just lay in ruins; it was as if they were never there. Nothing remained but lunar-cratered raised garden beds where the hail had impacted and then melted away.

Home that evening, we were in shock. She felt like a hurricane victim and would not come outside the house for the next two days. I surveyed the damage. Vehicles had all been under cover and all of our ranch's roofs are metal, but hail had completely stripped the woodbine on the west side of our home and had flailed most of the paint off the barn roofs. Except for girdled limbs, the trees would struggle back and recover, and before fall I'd need to replace some windows for the chickens. The gardens were a total loss. We railed, exasperated, and cursed the climate: "The end of frost ushers in hail season which lasts until first frost in fall!"

Every year hail singes us some, but this was utter devastation. We could replant. It was still early June, but why replant? Surely more hail was on the way, she wept. And I'd thought that it was just squash . . . but it isn't just squash, just a garden. The garden is her prize, her crown jewel of her favorite season of summer. She waits all winter for gardening—planning the beds and the crops.

In life I've learned that worry and depression are awfully poor substitutes for action. Circumstances can get me down as they do anyone, but I am not one to be daunted. Gathering myself internally, I rallied. I faced her, squeezing her hands in mine and said, "I will fix this."

"We always have some hail, but never this bad, never. This is the kick in the butt we needed. I'm going to build us some kind of garden coffee tables, hail tables. Something to stop this yearly sorrow." She wondered what such tables would be. I wasn't sure myself, but we needed them. Something to stand above and protect wide garden beds and broad green leaves, fragile as tissue paper. Something to break the hurtling plummet of thousands of ice balls from forty thousand feet above. Yet the tables would have to let sun and rain through. They would have to be big and strong enough to cover a lot of garden and yet not be terribly expensive. They'd need to be light-weight and permanent too, as I'd like to be troubled with building them only once. Hmm . . . Two by fours would not do. They'd dry out and fall apart and would make a frame too heavy to move over a garden patch. No landscape fabric on top either, it's too dark. Chicken wire wouldn't work. The sun and rain but also the hail would come right through.

After much discussion, I resolutely rolled out the gas welder and set to work welding lightweight "electrician's hail tables" out of half-inch thin walled galvanized steel electrical conduit. The four legs, their bottoms pinched shut, are thirty inches tall and support a tubing framework for a five-foot-wide by ten-foot-long reinforcing wire table that is then covered in quarter-inch hardware cloth. Perfect for the job, we hoped.

Welding thin tubing can be tricky and the hot sun had sweat rivulets running behind my welding goggles into my eyes. Labor intensive to be sure, but slowly the hail tables began to take shape. They weren't all complete when the next storm hit.

This storm was not as large as the previous one, five weeks before, but it was fast moving, full of lightning and hail. Alarmed, I threw plastic lawn furniture over the re-planted back garden and ran to the house. My steps were urged on by deafening thunder as lightning struck very close, all around. Rain came in a rush, icy cold and seeming to pelt down in a stinging rebuke. Then came the hail. As evening darkness conspired to cloak the storm's mischief I could see white ice balls frozen in mid-air by blinding strobe flashes of lightning.

Where was she? The storm had come upon us with such rapid ferocity, I wasn't sure. Concerned, the fury of the burgeoning storm kept me from searching or calling out. I strode to the study to watch from safety as the storm hammered down on our front garden. The garden's re-planted squash had leaves, eight inches wide

Rain came in a rush, icy cold and seeming to pelt down in a stinging rebuke.

Then came the hail.

waving lazily in intensifying cold down drafts. She had been watching too, from safety on the other side of the yard. And then it came. The small hail gave way to marble-sized hail following the rain, hammering the land and splashing in the sheet flooding in our front yard.

Two just-completed prototype hail tables, five feet wide by ten feet long were in place over the front garden. As I watched the booming storm from safety I worried. Would the storm blow them over? But their legs were pressed firmly into the earth and the tables were wired together, end to end. Would quarter-inch hardware cloth, just big window screen really—be able to withstand the punishing hail?

Cold down blasts brought small stones that stuck in the wire, then came the big ones, the garden shredders. Hail roared down like the applause of thousands, like a fast freight train passing over our home's metal roof. Out in the garden on top of the tables the hail first bounced, hopped and then strangely began dancing. Marble-sized stones looked like nothing but happy energetic popcorn, hopping and jumping in their hundreds upon the quarter-inch screen just above the squash. Beneath the wire, large delicate leaves waved lazily, as big Hawaiian palm fronds might on a breezy tropical day. Success! As we had hoped, the garden was oblivious to the storm.

> **Hail roared down like the applause of thousands, like a fast freight train passing over our home's metal roof.**

That fast moving storm roared on by to share its hail with our neighbors to the east. The storm eerily shut off as abruptly as it had started. She ran to me from her shelter across the yard, as I ran to her splashing through bobbing hail stones in the sheet flood. "They work! They work!" She wept, her forehead pinched and pressed into my chest. Tears were streaming down her cheeks and she began laughing convulsively at the same time and clutched my waist in her arms.

That fall there were vegetables in our root cellar. So even hail-filled clouds have a silver lining. I remember basking in her countenance and visceral joyous relief, her hero once again. ❃

Eat at Joel's by Paul Spielman

No Compost, No Digestion

A chapter excerpt from Joel Salatin's book, *Folks, This Ain't Normal*

Food that won't rot just ain't normal. Throughout history, our living food enjoyed the distinct ability to rot. Not until canning, and then freezing, did preservation develop beyond drying, smoking, curing (pork), or lacto-fermenting.

Even food preserved in this way will rot once it's taken out of its protected state. If you hydrate dried fruit, for example, it will get moldy, eventually sour, and then rot. Parched corn dried down in an oven or a solar drier, when rehydrated, will mold and then turn to sour mash.

If Teresa sends me to our basement stash of home-canned vegetables, venison, and pickles with a shopping list, a nonsealed jar will sport a healthy crop of white mold and we feed it to the chickens. If we leave frozen meat out too long in the thawing process, it will get slimy, then smell fishy, then begin rotting right before our eyes. Food's ability to rot is one of the historically normal protections to keep us from eating spoiled fare.

Curing bacon with salt and pepper became a mainstay of Virginia agriculture during the 1700s. Home-curing pork before refrigeration required temperature fluctuations that Virginia's fall climate delivered more dependably than any other bioregion. The fresh pork must stay cold enough to not spoil until it can absorb the salt. It can't freeze or the juices will quit flowing inside the meat. The juices are the cure's conduit into the muscle tissue.

North of Virginia the climate was too cold and freezing too likely to entrust the precious pork to natural curing. South of Virginia the cold was too unpredictable to keep the meat from spoiling before it absorbed the cure. That is why Virginia became the leading state for cured pork. It wasn't because pigs liked Virginia, or that Virginians especially liked pork. It was because in the days before environmentally controlled storage, Virginia's cool nights and warm days in the fall provided just the right mix to dependably cure pork.

But even that pork, if unwrapped and exposed for very long, would begin to rot. Rotting is decomposition, which is nature's recycling program. If something won't rot, or decompose, we usually call it something other than food. It's plastic or metal or stone. And while those things do degrade, they don't rot in a biological sense;

they erode or rust or break down into a more basic molecular structure.

Many years ago I remember reading an article about a farm unable to compost feedlot manure because it didn't have enough microbes in it to decompose. The manure was rendered virtually sterile with all the parasiticides, antibiotics, and other additives in the cattle diet. To be sure, manure that won't decompose is entirely abnormal.

Many years ago we had extra grass going into winter and didn't have enough cows to eat it all. We negotiated a deal with a neighbor to winter his cows at our place on a per diem basis. Not wanting to cause us any problems, he wormed them with a parasiticide before bringing the herd over to our farm in the fall. Our normal protocol required following the cows with our Eggmobile, a portable laying hen house that allows the chickens to range free behind the herbivores. This biomimicry duplicates the natural pattern obvious the world over wherein birds sanitize behind herbivores, scratching through their dung, eating out fly larvae, and spreading out the dung for more rapid decomposition.

> The life, death, decomposition, regeneration cycle is both physically and ecologically fundamental and profoundly spiritual.

A cow pie doesn't last long in our pastures. Those chickens go for fat fly larvae like kids to gourmet gelato. Within moments of letting the chickens out of their Eggmobile in the morning, they find and obliterate cow pies in a mad dash to this delectable buffet.

When this new herd of cows arrived at our farm, I was concerned about what they might bring, so I decided to move the Eggmobile away from our small herd and run it behind these new arrivals. Just precautionary. I knew what was in our cow pies, but these foreign pies might have aliens in them. I certainly didn't want any of that. So I sent in the chickens.

They wouldn't touch the cow pies. Used to attacking these pies, they simply looked askance, cocking their heads from one side to another, clearly sizing up what looked fairly normal, but then invariably backed away as if the pies contained poison. Amazed, I assumed something was going on that I couldn't see. Give it time, I reasoned. The second day yielded the same result. And day three. All the way through the week.

> ## We've all seen reports of drilling down through landfills. Hot dogs decades old and hundreds of feet deep rise to the bore surface and are perfectly edible.

I couldn't believe it. Had my chickens suddenly decided to express their chickenness differently? Had they suddenly forgotten the most fundamental principle of chickenhood? I decided on day eight to move the Eggmobile back behind our little herd and check out this unprecedented phenomenon. Wonder of wonders! The second I opened the doors, the chickens descended their ladders and attacked the cow pies, with more than normal vengeance to make up for lost time. Their exuberance was palpable as they scattered, scratched, and pecked. "Oh, goody, goody," they seemed to say, "we're back to edible pies."

After a couple of days, I took them back to the foreign cows. Same thing. I brought the Eggmobile back behind our cows—oh happy day! Welcome to the world of sterile poop. Now, folks, I'm no scientist, but I guarantee you that any cow pie that won't make a chicken salivate with delight just ain't normal. It makes me want to create a new farm mantra: "As for me and my poop, we will taste delicious to chickens."

Life is not sterile. Biology is not sterile. Things that won't rot, or won't decompose, or a disposal system that impairs decomposition, all characterize inanimate things, mechanical things. We are surrounded, inside and outside, with bacteria and decomposition. The entire principle of recycling hinges on the ability of something to decompose. Imagine if when things died they did not decompose. Leaves, grass, carcasses of bugs and animals. Trees that fall over. The life, death, decomposition, regeneration cycle is both physically and ecologically fundamental and profoundly spiritual.

When we masticate that carrot between our teeth, we are taking the life of that carrot, crushing it, flooding it with bacteria-laden saliva, and decomposing it in our own bodies, with our own microbial community, which extracts new life from it and builds cells in our bodies, bone of our bone and flesh of our flesh. The spiritual metaphor is powerful: Without sacrifice, life cannot exist. Whether it's plant or animal, something must give its life for life to occur.

That so many religious sacraments and rites revolve around foods indicates a historic appreciation for the death-life reality. It also reflects a deep-seated understanding that food is fundamentally living. It is not inert protoplasm, but a biological entity, fully living and lifegiving. It is fragile. Leave it exposed to the elements and very shortly it will begin to rot, or decompose.

That our culture has landfilled millions of tons of food wastes, and continues to do so, without a respectful decomposition protocol bespeaks a great irreverence for life. In previous cultures, no peels, cores, or uneaten food would be disposed of in a way that denied that life the opportunity to become life for something else. We've all seen reports of drilling down through landfills. Hot dogs decades old and hundreds of feet deep rise to the bore surface and are perfectly edible. So far, nobody really knows how long it will take for these food scraps and decomposable waste to become life again.

If you include yard waste and wood products in the percentage of decomposable inputs to landfills, it accounts for roughly 75 percent. That is immoral. To deny all that life a chance to decompose and restart the life cycle is not only insensitive, it is ecologically reprehensible. That material, had it all been encouraged to rot, could have fed the soil and maintained fertility without the use of toxic nonbiological petroleum-based fertilizers. It's not that we don't have enough biomass to maintain life; we have simply squandered the treasures given to us by solar energy and photosynthesis.

I recently spoke at a foodie conference in a big city and a lady, visibly torn with angst and frustration, asked, "I'm in an apartment. Every day I fret over how to dispose of my kitchen scraps. Do you know how hard it is to get rid of kitchen scraps in a city apartment complex?" What is easy for us on the farm is quite another story in the city.

That is why I advocate getting rid of the parakeet cage and replacing it with a couple of chickens. They are much quieter and far more industrious. They wouldn't require any more space than a fifty-gallon aquarium. How many households have an aquarium? Every time I get on this soapbox people begin laughing, and I realize it's a bit out of the box, but I'm absolutely serious about this.

Barring the chickens, get a vermicomposting kit. They are not expensive and quite sophisticated. In a contraption no larger than half a dozen shoe boxes, you can feed your kitchen scraps to worms and enjoy pathogen-free, nutrient-rich earthworm castings for your houseplants. If you don't have any houseplants, store the sweet-smelling fertility in a breathable bag and wait for your next trip to a farmers' market. I'm sure you can find a farmer more than willing to take the black gold off your hands.

I think farmers' markets should have food scrap receptacles so their customers can deposit this waste. Farmers could take it home and feed it to their chickens, or add it to their compost piles. Please understand, never before in human history have food scraps been placed anywhere they couldn't decompose and add fertility to the soil. Never. Putting it in plastic, carting it all over creation, and finally depositing it in anaerobic landfills where it can lie in state for centuries is not only abnormal, it's an ecological travesty.

While we're on the urban challenge—which occurs in lots of areas, from children's gardens to this composting issue—it's easy to start spluttering, "But, but, but what about?" I confess, I don't have all the answers. I know that's disappointing, but in full disclosure, I don't purport to have it all figured out. When I talk about cooking, people invariably bring up the single working mom with no time. When I talk about buying nutrient-dense food, people challenge me with, "What if someone can't afford that kind of food?"

If I mention gardens, the response is quick: "I don't have any land." On this one, composting or worm bins or two chickens, some will argue that they don't have room or time or whatever. "I can't have pets in my apartment" puts the kibosh on the chickens. Are earthworms considered pets? I don't think so.

I do a lot of speaking and these peripheral "what ifs" always come up to challenge my harebrained solutions. Right here, right now, I admit that I don't have the

answer to all the fringes. When farmers in Idaho who live a hundred miles from a Coke machine ask me about selling local, I don't have a cookie-cutter plan.

With all this in mind, though, instead of picking away at the edges and challenging with the most fringe possibility, why don't we focus on the great majority for whom the idea is doable? Instead of saying my ideas are stupid because not everybody has land or room for a

chicken yard, how about realizing how many people living on city lots, in the suburbs, or rural farmettes don't do any of this stuff? The truth is that if the majority would do the innovative right thing, the culture would change so dramatically we probably can't even conceive what the next tweaking would look like.

If all the households that could afford nutrient-dense food grew a garden, discovered their kitchen—would actually do these things—it would fundamentally return our food system to a state of normalcy. At that point, answers for the fringes would be more apparent. Step four doesn't look as forbidding once we've taken steps one, two, and three. I submit that we haven't even taken step one on most of these solutions. I'm not suggesting we should plunge willy-nilly into the unknown without planning, but can anyone think of a reason why people in the suburbs shouldn't grow their own food? Or raise some chickens and rabbits? Or have a chest freezer for bulk purchases? These are not dangerous ideas—unless you're the CEO of an industrial food system. Then they are downright subversive.

My dad was quite an innovator, and when he'd design a new machine or a system, we kids would begin with the "what ifs." Rather than answering each one, I can well remember him laughing and responding, "Well, we're going to know a lot more in thirty minutes than we do right now." What a wonderful outlook. He was saying that although he didn't have it all figured out, the right thing to do is to proceed immediately with the best plan according to current information. It'll work itself out as we move and adjust, move and adjust.

If nobody can move until everybody can, we'll never move. If we have to know every contingency before we move, we have the proverbial paralysis by analysis. The truth is that if everyone who could do what is noble and right would do it now, the cultural shift would be like an epic earthquake. And that would make room for the next set of changes. Defending our own intransigence to

> ## Reducing spoilage through fermentation, vacuum sealing, drying, or freezing is both normal and ancient. What is new is food marketed as edible that will not rot at all in its consumable state.

change by pointing out the desperate state of those who can't is simply irresponsible at best and negligent at worst. We can make excuses until the cows come home. What we need to do is be faithful with what we know until the cows show up. They may show up and they may not, but we have a job list right now. Let's get at it. Living food, decomposing kitchen scraps, and living soil should be incorporated into everyone's life. Let's get at it.

Lest anyone think life doesn't exist in the soil, let me explain the real world under our feet. This is not just inert material that elicits a "Yuck" and a capful of detergent in the washing machine. It is a living, vibrant community so populous that in one double handful of healthy soil more individual life exists than there are people on the face of the earth. And that's just one double handful.

Let's see this world come to life under the magnification of the electron microscope: Wandering into the viewscape, a six-legged grazing microbe, lollygagging along on hairlike cilia, comes into view. Without warning, a nautilus-looking four-legged predator rockets in from two o'clock, impales the grazer with the saberlike spear affixed to its head, and sucks out the juices from the soft belly of the grazer. Before the hapless grazer microbe can fall to the hairy pasture, however, another predator enters the viewscape from ten o'clock and lops off the grazer's head, devouring it contentedly as the now-decapitated and fluid-deflated carcass hits the ground. Within moments, other smaller scavengers enter

the viewscape and polish off the carcass crumbs.

This is all in a normal moment of activity in the soil. It makes Steven Spielberg's imagination look like a kindergartner. Better than sci-fi, better than Dr. Seuss, this real world of microbial soil life plays out the life-death-life drama every moment of every day. Yet most of us go through our days never pausing to even contemplate that our bodies, our very existence, our breath and being, are absolutely and completely dependent on this unseen world.

Lest anyone think I'm heading toward a dissertation of animism or paganism, or even romanticism, I am not. Rather, I see a divine hand in this complex intricacy—this marvelous, mystical, microscopic world—and fall to my knees in humility. Traditional and indigenous Eastern-styled peoples around the world maintain this reverence that connects all of us to an ecological umbilical. Our complete powerlessness to live, to do, without the active participation of this unseen microbial recycling and regenerative community should infuse us with awe and respect toward soil and food as a living substance. The visible, touchable, hearable world is literally tethered to a vibrant, moving, communicating, interacting, relational invisible community foundation.

And so we come to the crux of the matter: Whatever happened to food that rots? A mere century ago, not only did all food scraps get reused through the chickens or pigs, but you couldn't place something on a table and have it sit there indefinitely without decaying. Even table wine, if exposed to the air, soon deteriorates. Root cellaring is an ancient preservation technique, but it only lasts a few months. Those vegetables, when brought into the house, will begin to deteriorate in a couple of days.

Reducing spoilage through fermentation, vacuum sealing, drying, or freezing is both normal and ancient. What is new is food marketed as edible that will not rot at all in its consumable state. I met a fellow at a conference who told me he had a burger museum in his house. He said he has purchased one burger every year for twenty years from a particular fast food chain that will remain anonymous for obvious litigious reasons. The burgers have not changed significantly in all that time. They don't shrink appreciably, don't mold, don't rot. They just sit there, looking perfect. Day after day after day.

Think about the things in your kitchen and your pantry. Will they spoil if you don't eat them soon? The most notorious offenders are junk foods. Many varieties of candy can last virtually indefinitely. How long do kids hoard their Halloween stash in their rooms? Months?

Several years ago we participated in a food fair and wanted to illustrate the differences between our meat and its industrial counterpart. We went to the supermarket and bought a pound of ground beef and cooked it into burgers. We cooked a pound of ours into burgers. We measured the grease, put it in jars, and took the burgers to the fair. The cooking loss on the industrial burgers was significant compared to ours. When people complain about food costs for real food, they don't appreciate how much more nutritious the real deal is.

The fair was outside and on a warm day. When everything was done for the day, we didn't want to throw the burgers away so we took them home. We had four cats at the time—our biological vermin control unit—and just for fun, I put the four burgers from the supermarket on one plate and the Polyface grass-fed burgers on another plate. The four cats came running when I set the plates down on the back porch. I purposely put the supermarket burgers closest to the cats so they would come to that plate first.

The cats approached the supermarket burgers, sniffed, and then stepped right over them to the other plate with the Polyface burgers on it. They devoured every one of those burgers, licked the plate clean, and refused to touch the supermarket burgers. I tell this story partly because it's a good story, but mainly because most people feel powerless to really verify the claims about food integrity that people like me expound. Most people just can't believe that in our enlightened culture we could actually be consuming bad food.

After all, if it's junk, shouldn't it be illegal? I mean, if someone adulterates the gasoline going into our car, heads will roll. Nobody is going to mess up my engine. But when it comes to food, not only are we pouring junk into our bodies' engines, we don't seem to care when we blow a gasket. Like blowing a gasket is supposed to be common or something. If our car engine blows a gasket, all our friends come around sympathetically offering condolences and we enjoy being depressed together. But if our bodies have an equivalent breakdown, we assume we've been the victim of faulty genes or the disease fairies, sprinkling their disease whimsically from the heavens.

This cat burger story, then, is a simple way for you to check me out. Don't take my word for it. Go duplicate this with your own cats. They are not funded by industrial food conglomerates. They don't have political alliances. They are not peer-dependent or swayed by hours of TV advertising. They are just primal beings whose sensory safeguards still function. Indeed, your pets probably have a much better handle on nutrition than your doctor. So ask your cats. Do the test. Folks, cat-repugnant burgers are not normal. If the cats don't want them, what do you think about your intestinal bacteria? What about the decomposers?

Think about compost. You put in wood chips, manure, grass clippings, banana peels, and wood ashes, and in a matter of days it takes on a completely different look. You can't distinguish the parent materials. It doesn't smell like the individual components you put in.

> . . . if it's junk, shouldn't it be illegal? I mean, if someone adulterates the gasoline going into our car, heads will roll. Nobody is going to mess up my engine. But when it comes to food, not only are we pouring junk into our bodies' engines, we don't seem to care when we blow a gasket.

It becomes homogeneous, dark, earthy, full of worms, bugs, beetles, and creepy-crawlies. Where did they come from? How did the initial raw ingredients turn into this? It is a completely different substance. This, dear friends, is death come to life.

If you put raw milk on the kitchen table in the morning, it will spoil by evening. You can smell and taste the spoilage. Ditto for raw meat, poultry, or eggs. But what about ultra-pasteurized milk? Touted as a way to extend shelf life, this procedure inhibits life-giving, life-necessitating decomposition—could we even say it destroys the sacrifice necessary for life? I know this is flirting with profound spiritual truth, but one thing I believe very strongly is that truth, real truth, permeates and threads its way seamlessly through the physical and spiritual. If it doesn't work spiritually, it won't work physically. And if it won't work physically, it won't work spiritually.

A homemade pound cake, made with real raw ingredients, will only last at household ambient temperature for a couple of days before white mold spots start dotting its exterior. That is why I eat this pound cake quickly and aggressively—immediate consumption is my personal preservation policy toward pound cakes.

But no, it is not preservation, it is death, decomposition, and new life. Especially around my love handles. But see how long an industrial supermarket pound cake lasts out on the kitchen counter. Days. Weeks. It just sits there.

Think about the difference between homemade bread and the industrial supermarket counterpart. Who puts white bread in the refrigerator? Nobody does. You just leave it out on the counter and it stays perfectly edible for days. But if you use real flour, or especially if you grind your flour and then bake the bread, it will begin to mold within twenty-four hours. That doesn't mean the bread is poorly made.

On the contrary, it indicates that the homemade bread is full of life. And only fully alive things can decompose with virility enough to then resurrect in us a fully vibrant life. We as people can only be as vibrant as the vitality in the food we've decomposed in our digestive system. If that food went in lifeless, it doesn't have anything left to give, to create in us new cells, new flesh, new bones. This is such a basic intuitive principle that corroborative science, while it may be interesting, should not be required to convince us of such an essential principle. And yet our whole food processing industry cranks out product after product that won't rot.

How long will a candy bar sit out before it goes bad? A pastry with a sell-by date of a year hence is not real food at all. It may be ingestible, but it certainly won't rot. Instead of ingesting things that won't rot, we should all be devoted to eating only things that will rot. Cooked whole foods and casseroles need to be refrigerated right away. Why? Because they will rot.

You can check the viability of foods easily this way. Cheese is a good example. I challenge you: Put slices of Velveeta or liquid cheese out on the counter next to artisanal cheese. The real cheese will get moldy in a day or so. The other cheese will sit there for days without growing anything. If it won't grow anything, can it grow cells for you? Folks, we shouldn't need dieticians or nutritional therapists to tell us, "No!" This is not hard to understand. Yet if you look into the average shopping cart coming out of the supermarket today, very little will grow mold if exposed to air and ambient temperature for forty-eight hours.

We can all be grateful that vegetables and fruits, in their whole, unprocessed, raw state can hold up as long as they do. Otherwise, our predecessors before refrigeration would have had a tough time. As soon as we break the skin, peel, rind, or whatever, exposure initiates the decay process. As I think about these principles, it occurs to me that perhaps God—my preference, or if you prefer, nature, or Gaia, or the cosmos—designed things this way to give us a litmus test on what to eat. If we didn't know, how could we know? We could know by looking at the decay cycle. If it would grow mold quickly, it was edible. Stated another way, if it would decompose, it was food. If not, like a stick or a stone, it was not edible. If today we would return to such a test, it would eliminate way more than half of the food ingested by Americans.

To think that we can devitalize—you can read that as disrespect—food life to this degree and then have a healthy population is insane. No civilization can be healthier than the life energy in the food it eats. And even more fundamentally, no society can be economically or ecologically healthier than the soil on which it depends. A bankrupt soil policy will naturally create a bankrupt food system will inevitably create a bankrupt health reality. No nation can be healthier than its soil-food life.

Processing in modern America seems devoted to making food lifeless. Taking out nutrients and then adding synthetics creates what is euphemistically called shelf life. Not much life about it. More like embalming a cadaver and calling it body extension. If we're going to stay true to digestive bacteria, we need to eat things that will perish. In order to perish, they need to be living. If they aren't living, they can't perish. If they can't perish, they can't give life. Contrary to most popular thinking, perishability is really a good thing, not a bad thing. The next time you buy any food, just put it out on the kitchen counter for a couple of days. If it doesn't significantly change in appearance, taste, odor, or texture, you just wasted your money on dead stuff. Except for when it's dehydrated, living food at ambient temperature has a relatively short existence. Living food is normal food.

> To think that we can devitalize — you can read that as disrespect — food life to this degree and then have a healthy population is insane. No civilization can be healthier than the life energy in the food it eats.

What can we do?

1. Resolve today to keep kitchen wastes on your premises with animals, worms, or compost. Don't send it down the garbage disposal or out onto the curb with the rest of the trash. Separate and nourish the earth with its own blanket of biomass.

2. Institutional food services have the same imperative. On our farm, we've tried to get our restaurants to separate their food scraps so we can bring them home—go loaded with edibles and return home loaded with animal food — but so far have made no real progress. This must change.

3. If in doubt about your food, set it out for a couple of days and see if it will grow mold. If it doesn't, quit buying it. Buy only perishable food.

4. The one stable food at ambient temperature is dehydrated items and nuts. Rehydrating the dried food should make it grow mold. Nuts are the best exception to all these rules—and delicious to eat. ❁

This is an excerpt from FOLKS, THIS AIN'T NORMAL by Joel Salatin. Copyright © 2011 by Joel Salatin. Reprinted by permission of Center Street. All rights reserved.

Bulbs A vintage illustration by Joseph E. Ebertz

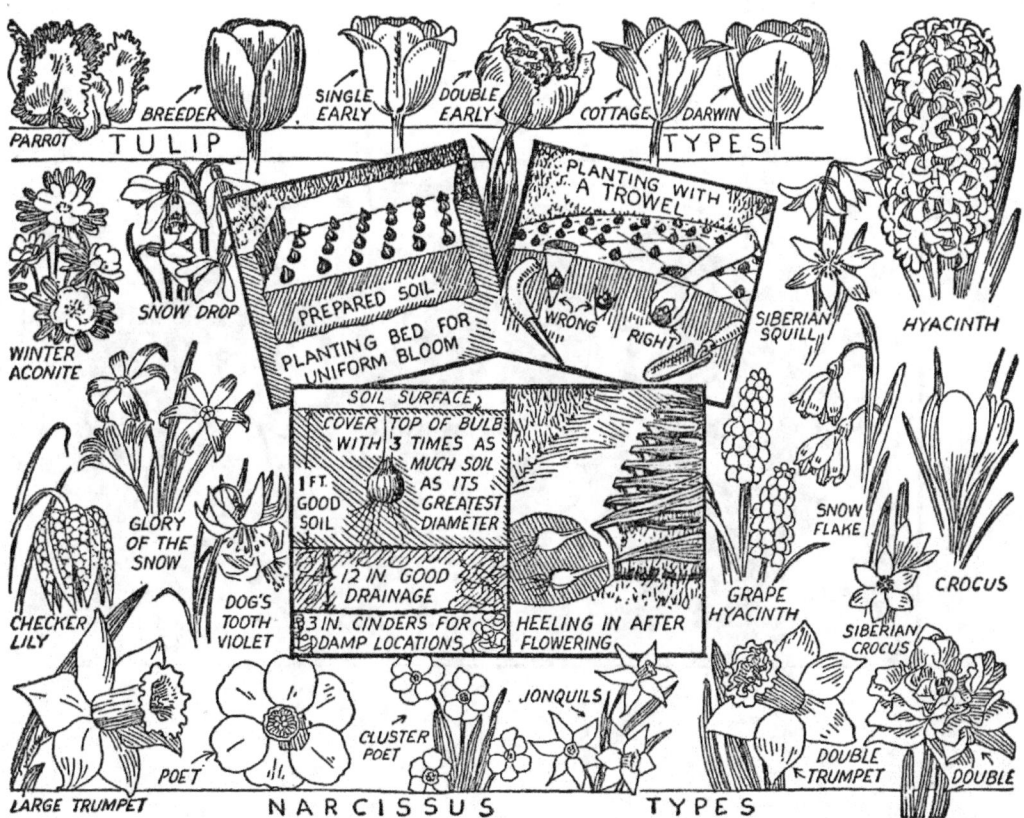

Garden Relatives

by Jane Knechtel

Gather to say farewell:
Our maple weeping like a child.
The dogwood as resigned as a grandparent.
Roses climbing the walls, moodier than debutantes.
Lone worms going to pieces;
Crows shrieking their disapproval—
Seeds clinging.

Harvest

by Kathryn Kulpa

She finds him in the early morning, kneeling in the ruined garden where, the night before, her headlights had startled a fox. Reina had seen the flashbulb glare of its eyes, seen it turn and dash through the bushes, not quite seen something fall from its mouth. Owen has the shovel. It was a rabbit, he says.

Reina is glad he's been the undertaker for the rabbit and all the field mice their cat has brought to the back door and lined up in neat rows, heads facing the house, tails facing away. Ritual arrangement of bodies, the sign of a true serial killer, Owen said. He asked the cat to wish the mice into a grave in the cornfield, but she only gave a long, slow blink.

Owen stands up, bracing himself against the shovel. His knee is still wobbly from the accident. He does that thing with his lip, rubbing the back of his thumb against it, pressing his thumbnail into the small indentation under his nose. He does it when he's worried or lost in thought. It was something she noticed soon after they'd met. Lately she thinks that hollow above his mouth is starting to get deeper, worn down from all that thumb-pressing.

Owen wipes his hands across dirt-stained Levis. "We should take this all out," he says, nodding at the crumbling leaves, the tomato plants that long ago overgrew their stakes. Most of them never ripened, just stayed green until they turned pulpy and soft. Here are the spinach plants chewed to ragged stalks; here are the herbs Reina planted and never used. She planted them because she liked their names: rosemary, that's for remembrance, and rue. What is rue for?

In another life she would have learned to cook. Owen has been talking about places they could go if they lose the house: a trailer in his friend Jake's yard, a boot factory some group had turned into a housing unit for artists. He doesn't talk about his parents' house, although his mother had called Reina last week: You know our door is open. In another life they would stay here forever. Owen would build Adirondack chairs. She would have a kitchen garden. She would have a pear tree. She would gather honeycombs and make rosemary honey.

"Don't we have zucchini and summer squash?" Reina asks.

"They're all soft," he says. "Frost-killed."

Isn't it too early for frost? Reina looks down at her feet in flip-flops, toes more violet than rose. She'll have to start wearing real shoes now, though she hates them. She'll have to start pulling sweaters and corduroys from the storage bins under the bed. She sees a brave red between the brown vines and pulls a tomato. The top is shiny and the fruit is firm in her hand, and she's sure the black spots on the bottom don't matter. She holds it out. Owen reaches for it, but his eyes don't leave the ground.

"It's still good," she says. ✻

Modern Homemaker VICTORY RECIPE EDITION, 1942, *Greenwoman* Collection

Oh, Ophidia!
The Creature Feature by DB Rudin

I *walk through the Lacandon rainforest in the state of Chiapas, in southern Mexico. My Mayan guide Elisario swings a machete, clearing trail, ten yards ahead. Since Spanish is a second language for both of us, the chit-chat is kept to a minimum.*

Suddenly Elisario yells and streaks by me on a dead run. The words, "Serpiente Grande!" trail as he passes. I feel like I am in a Tarzan movie. Of course the logical thing to do is to run after the guy with the machete. For me it is an invitation to run the opposite way, fumbling with my camera as I go. What I see stops me dead in my tracks. The biggest snake I have ever encountered is raising its head three feet in the air, right in the middle of the trail, looking straight at me. He is as thick as my forearm, ten feet long so help me, the front two-thirds a dark grey, the back third a yellow-orange. He stares at me, flicking his tongue, trying to make out what I am. As I resume trying to surreptitiously ready my camera, he turns and vanishes in a flash, down a hole under a tree.

Gone! I am shocked that such a large animal can move with such speed.

The adrenaline rush of this encounter has only added to my lifelong fascination with these creatures.

Most gardeners are unlikely to run into a *Cribo* (a non-venomous species and relative of the southwestern U.S. Indigo snake I'd find out later), but many people shun even the innocuous members of the snake tribe. These creatures have become some of the most successful predators on the planet, evolving into nearly 3,000 species, all without arms or legs. How they came to be this way is a fantastic tale in its own right.

Snakes belong to the sub-order *Serpentes* or *Ophidia*, from the Greek *Ophis* meaning "serpent." Herpetologists, scientists who study amphibians and reptiles, commonly believe that snakes evolved from monitor-like lizards. Monitors are the family of lizards which include the seemingly prehistoric Komodo Dragon. It might be helpful to think of snakes, then, as an unusually large and successful group of legless lizards. ("True" legless lizards usually have eyelids and external ear openings while snakes do not.) Leglessness has actually evolved several times amongst lizards. The Eastern Glass Lizard lives in the southeastern United States. The glass part of its name is because its tail fractures into pieces, like glass, when attacked by a predator. This successful strategy allows the lizard to escape and grow a new tail another day, while the predator is left holding a few wriggling pieces of lizard appendage.

As they lived underground and often used tiny invertebrate tunnels, legs only got in the way, so they disappeared over time.

Scientists have pieced together a remarkable story of how these creatures evolved into their present forms. As snakes fossilize poorly, the detective work is all the more challenging and the conclusions more controversial. Here are the rough and ready highlights of one theory:

Some especially enterprising little lizards, somewhere around 100 million years ago, found a plentiful food supply underground. Invertebrates (animals like worms and insects that lack a backbone) of various kinds lived there, sometimes in colonies. This food source also had the advantage of keeping the lizards safe from the dominant above-ground predators of the time, namely dinosaurs.

As they lived underground and often used tiny invertebrate tunnels, legs only got in the way, so they disappeared over time. Eyes were an unnecessary waste of energy in a dark world, so they went too, leaving vestigial remnants used to differentiate light from dark. What was indispensable in this ecosystem niche was a means of tracking down their prey as well as others of their kind. So they evolved an incredibly acute chemo-sensory system featuring a forked tongue which sampled its surroundings for chemical clues.

Around 65 million years ago the dinosaurs met their demise when a large asteroid crashed into earth. (Some of those dinosaurs survived and became birds.) For some great background on this event check out the *Smithsonian*'s piece: http://paleobiology.si.edu/dinosaurs/info/everything/why.html.

The great age of mammals had begun.

The next part of the story is the most speculative. Perhaps, tempted by this moveable feast of mammals and birds, some of these enterprising subterranean "snakes," now blind and limbless, came back to the dinosaur-less surface and over millions of years evolved into the thousands of species of snakes we now know today.

The theory is that they re-evolved their eyes from the vestigial remnants used for a life in the dark but, curiously enough, did not re-evolve limbs. Perhaps they found it an advantage moving through certain types of terrain. Anyone who has ever seen a snake disappear effortlessly in thick grass can see that advantage.

The process of evolution had only just begun. Snakes have since evolved into a myriad of species of varying sizes and dietary preferences. All are carnivores. Queen snakes of the southeast US specialize in eating crayfish, but only those who have just recently molted their exoskeleton. All the better to digest them! Some tiny blind snakes, the size of earthworms, still live a subterranean existence on a diet of insects and their larvae. Then there are the true behemoths—python and boa families that grow to over 20 feet, weigh hundreds of pounds and count antelope and even small humans as dietary options. They use constriction to subdue their meals. Finally, the most infamous group; those who have forsaken the rough and tumble of constricting prey and instead use venom. It is for these serpents that humans save their strongest fears and disdain.

Studies have been done that show young primates who, without any previous exposure to snakes, will react fearfully to them or even unknown snake-shaped objects. It seems that fear of snakes may be hard-wired into some species. Stories like Adam and Eve haven't helped snake public relations either, though amongst Hindu and Mayan cultures snakes enjoy a place of reverence and worship. In Greek mythology, the Rod of Asklepios, a staff with a serpent entwined around it, is associated with healing and medicine. Ironically, it is the vilified venomous snakes who are now providing researchers with breakthroughs in cancer research as they analyze the compounds found in venom.

Venomous snakes are the exception, however. Most snakes typically found in our gardens are harmless. In fact snakes, like the two dozen odd species of garter snake, are beneficial to the garden, eating insects, slugs and even small rodents. They are often mistakenly called garden(er) snakes, but their true name derives from the stripes down their backs, reminiscent of another time when women wore garters with similar stripes. Being aware of where one puts ones hands, especially when moving rocks or logs, goes a long way towards avoiding surprise snake encounters.

Snakes add dimension to our world if we allow them, whether an adrenalin-producing surprise or just a quiet moment of observation. Snakes have truly made an evolutionary voyage worthy of song and story. So the next time you encounter a snake in your garden, try remembering their epic journey to a life without limbs.

Epilogue:

In another rainforest, this time in Costa Rica, a group of tourists walk behind me along a trail covered in leaves. I stop and stick out my arm to halt the procession. Sitting almost perfectly camouflaged in the middle of the trail is a tiny Hognosed Rainforest Pit Viper. Quite venomous. After the groups' expected gasps of fear, there is an intense curiosity. I can assure you no one looked at the jungle in the same light nor took their next step casually.

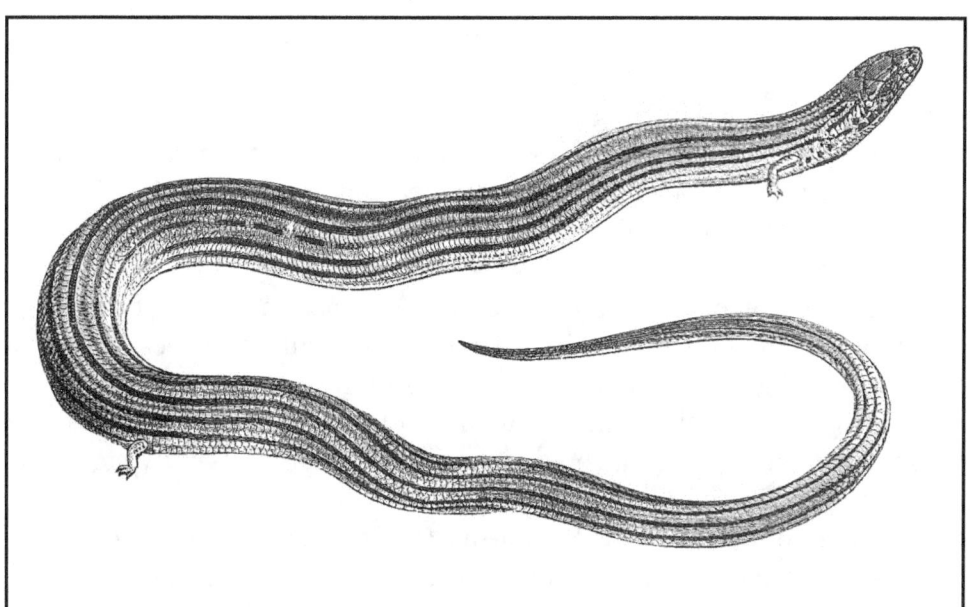

The Green Wasteland
by Sandra Knauf

My sister and I ended many summer afternoons in the 1970s green from the knees of our jeans down, sweaty, and reeking of gas and exhaust. As servants of the Great American Lawn, we regularly mowed ours, the elderly Miss Howard's next door, our grandma's, and once in a while, our great Aunt Flora's.

It was work that was necessary and our lawn in particular was well used—our family of six kids played games of tag, pitch and catch, badminton, and used the space, as teenagers, for sunbathing. Dad saw physical labor as the best character-builder, so he "volunteered" us. We received $5 a lawn, to share.

I didn't mind the work but Missouri summers were hot and humid, and occasionally at Miss Howard's I ran over a toad (a horrifying thing).

I learned more about turf at age 20, verifying sales for a lawn-care company in Colorado Springs. I telephoned clients, confirming that they had joined our fertilizer/weed killer program, with insecticide and/or fungicide treatments as needed. With our help, their lawns would be the envy of the neighborhood!

Seduced by the American Ideal, we installed sod. For a while, it looked gorgeous, but without pampering, chemicals, or a sprinkler system, it deteriorated fast.

During our one-day training, we learned to instruct clients with pets to remove dog and cat bowls before spraying, as there had been pet deaths from tainted water. We also cautioned them to keep pets and people off the grass until the applications dried. It sickened me to realize that the men who drove the trucks and sprayed these toxins daily would inhale them, get them on their clothing, their skin, and bring these toxins home. I wondered why people would pay good money for lawns you wouldn't want a baby crawling on.

A decade later, as a college grad, mom, and hobby gardener, I had my own lawn—or, rather, weed/ native grass lot. Seduced by the American ideal, we installed sod in our backyard. For a while, it looked gorgeous; but without pampering, chemicals or a sprinkler system, it deteriorated fast. In Colorado, lawns require constant life support.

A few years later when I became a master gardener, I determined to get rid of ours. Bit by bit, with a tiny budget and lots of elbow grease, I created a garden instead—with fruit trees, herbs, flowers, native plants, sandstone paths, even a goldfish pond. I kept patches of grass/weeds for our dogs (and the occasional badminton game) and maintain them now with a reel mower, enjoying a good workout in the process. Our established garden requires much less maintenance than a lawn. I water once a week, deeply, and I do not water the grass/weeds at all.

I realize that turf is a multibillion-dollar U.S. industry (in Colorado it's our #1 cash crop) and many are wedded to the old ways. Lawns, those pretty green carpets, do have an aesthetic charm and they are good for sports. But they don't support butterflies, honeybees, birds, other wildlife, or much of anything else. Caring for one is the antithesis of green. Five percent of all our nation's air pollution comes from gas-powered lawn mowers. According to the Union of Concerned Scientists, one gas-powered mower, used for one hour, emits as much pollution as eight new cars, driven at 55 mph for the same time.

According to the EPA, Americans burn 800 million gallons of fuel each year trimming their lawns. Of this, 17 million gallons of fuel, mostly gasoline, are spilled each year while refueling lawn equipment.

This is more than the oil spilled by the Exxon Valdez. Fertilizer pollution is a huge problem, and lawns require significant water, yet another burden on our limited resources.

In addition, nearly 80 million pounds of pesticide active ingredients are used on U. S. lawns annually. The U.S. Fish and Wildlife Service reported that "homeowners use up to 10 times more chemical pesticides per acre on their lawns than farmers use on crops."

It's past time to see traditional lawns for what they have become: antiquated, wasteful, and harmful. I propose that we return to our roots—cottage gardens. Gardens assist nature on a meaningful scale, they are excellent outdoor classrooms/playgrounds for children and adults, and they can provide families with locally-grown food. You cannot grow luscious plums, pull up sweet carrots, snip chives for your potatoes (and grow potatoes, too), pick wildflower bouquets, or provide bird sanctuary or forage for honeybees with a grass lawn.

As the industrialized world races toward green living, homeowners everywhere can make a difference. It's easy; take up your shovel and start getting rid of your lawn. ❋

References: People Powered Machines, http://www.peoplepoweredmachines.com/faq-environment.htm; Environment and Human Health, Inc., http://www.ehhi.org/reports/lcpesticides/summary.shtml;

© Can Stock Photo/watamyr

Embrace Reel Life!

Earth Girls Aren't Easy by Laura Chilson

The Gardener's Dirty Mind
A Sex in the Garden Essay
by
Elisabeth Kinsey

On his way home from a campaign, Napoleon Bonaparte wrote his wife, "Dear Josephine, I will be arriving home in three days. Don't bathe . . ."

One of the dirtiest words in existence in the 1400s was "slut," describing this unfortunate creature as a "dirty, slovenly or an untidy woman." As I dream of the time I've spent in Colorado soil, fingers cracked, digging out the longest part of a dandelion root or picking purslane seedlings, one by one, like picking out gray hairs, I long for even that transference between weeds, soil, and the body. Am I a slut to the earth? Are gardeners mere sluts, wanton slaves to their soil? I wondered at other gardeners' relationships to dirt and its sullied beginnings.

Let's explore a "dirty" profile, find out where soil got a dirty name: My imaginary Victorian, let's call her Lady Catherine, has nothing to do. She stopped her needlework years ago. She dabbled in painting and could barely get enough orange on a canvas to make an orange before she bored of it. Her mouth resembles a geisha's pretty tied-up bow with the bottom lip too full and supple for anything other than kissing by wild princes (riding uncontrollably across craggy moors to save Lady Catherine from twisting her ankle, or, worse yet, ennui).

Underneath Lady Catherine's many bandaged breasts (corsets, etc.) and her large dress-hoops is a sensual being that Victorian society deemed "dirty" and which by deeming it so converted the world under the dress, and at every gardener's foot, as something unnatural. The most important virtue, in order to be of High Victorian society, as we all know from the scene when Scarlet is forced to show her grubby, working hands in *Gone With the Wind*, was to be the owner of a pale, lifeless hand that went limp and delicate in any suitor's grip. Then it was swept up under his nose for the lightest and most normal of kisses. But wait, was that tongue?!!! I'm sure it was, recoils Lady Catherine, as she whips her porcelain fingers from the suitor's lips. How dirty, she thinks. How invasive. How very naughty.

> Dirt got really dirty in the Victorian era, stripping anything having to do with soil from it, thus vanquishing all roots between the natural, oozing, procuring earth and the natural, oozing and procuring body.

Dirt got really dirty in the Victorian era, stripping anything having to do with soil from it, thus vanquishing all roots between the natural, oozing, procuring earth and the natural, oozing, and procuring body. You can read up on the era and its prude expectations of women by delving into any Austin or even Cooksin novel. Dirt existed, whether the Victorian prigs wanted it or not. Dirt will always prevail, regardless of moniker.

Who are we now, we tillers of the land, Gods and Goddesses with hands as roots, reaching and groping into the earth for its dark secrets, accidentally digging up a lost tulip bulb, finding coins from the 70s, extracting someone else's white landscaping rock to reveal a barren hardness that we must convert back to its humus soul? Dare we admit that we are, in fact, dirty minded? Have we entered into the truest scandal in gardendom?

And who ruined soil? There were just enough uber-sexual beings to keep the dirty connotation. A scandalous dirt fetish is recorded between a Victorian-era barrister and his scullery maid in Wellcome Collection's London exhibition last year which explored attitudes about dirt ("Dirt: The Filthy Reality of Everyday Life") London journalist Giovanna Dunmall wrote about the exhibit:

"Our 21st-century preoccupation with germs and cleanliness is clearly not a new one . . . There is hardly a dull moment in this exploration of filth . . . [for example] letters detailing the bizarre 40-year relationship, and eventual marriage, between barrister Arthur Munby and scullery maid Hannah Cullwick in Victorian London. The former had a thing for working-class women whose jobs involved hard, physical labour and there are photographs of Cullwick dressed as a chimney sweep or posing covered in soot and dirt."

Most who walked through the streets of London at the time were used to grime (perhaps being one with it or dying by it?) and some carried a perfumed kerchief or nosegay to cover the stench of foul conditions. So many maladies stemmed from "dirt" that it was easily equated with filth. Before penicillin and sanitary drainage, it was an honest mistake; however, in our current society, worries about getting dirty in the garden bed stifles soil's natural yearnings. When I speak to real gardeners, and this is from the beginner through the pro, they always mention how important it is to get their "hands in the soil." Especially after winter's thaw, spring stirs something in every gardener's soul. For me, I constantly check the surface of the yard, kick it with a toe. Does it divot, indent? I take a shoe off and dip my naked toe. Does it accept any entrance?

The different constitutions of loam, clay, sand, and organic matter implant themselves in my dreams so that I wake with their dark, dusky smell in the mornings, hoping I can get into the dirt. One gardener calls this tactile transfer a communication with the soil. Tamara Mahoney, long-time certified Colorado master gardener has this to say, "Nothing calms my nerves or relieves my stress more than getting my hands in the dirt for a little bit. I love fresh carrots just dug out of my garden and washed in the garden hose . . . they taste like the dirt they have been growing in. No store-bought carrot ever tastes as good!"

> I needed to find other dirty minds in the search for support. That's not hard when talking to gardeners.

Tasting the dirt is not the only vice we dirt worshipers have, but it's a good one. Patricia Hampl stands up for eating a peck of dirt (two gallons) in her memoir *A Romantic Education*. She wrote about her grandparent's dark and tuber-producing garden. "I ate dirt there. This is the first taste I remember." After dropping a jawbreaker around the corner, the owner had said, "Well, you have to eat a peck of dirt before you die. " After that, Hampl reflected on death and dirt and pictured herself without the proper amount. She ruminates, "So I ate dirt. I also ate it out of curiosity, putting it on my tongue like brown sugar and waiting hopelessly for it to melt."

Our society and the media continue to sell us alcohol and other toxic cleaners to rid our hands of germs. Gardening gloves, like the corset, hinder transference. To combat dirt's bad connotation, it's not enough to just commune with the soil. Chuck Rise of Soil Science of America writes about soil's healthy properties and that, ironically, many antibiotics come from soil. Under our feet, and indeed, in our hands as gardeners, we touch the key to existence itself. Rice asks us, "Did you know that there are more living individual organisms in a tablespoon of soil than there are people on the earth? A teaspoon of soil contains over 1 billion bacteria yet we know only 1%. The remaining 99% are unknown and contain a treasure trove of products." I have so many friends who are new to dirt and slowly succumb to its call, accepting the lure, and therefore scandal, into their lives, but jump into their soil too soon, without finding out what it will do first. One such gardener had bad luck. On the Laguna Dirt blog, Janine Robinson even admits defeat when she didn't gauge her soil correctly. Kind of like going out in the middle of winter in a spaghetti strap dress. Sure, you'll ensnare a dude, but what kind of dude will he be?

"I started a winter vegetable garden in early November, and blogged about how I built the raised bed on top of my concrete patio, using concrete block . . . I filled it with seedlings and seeds, but even after weeks of rain and warm temps, things barely grew. With the help of some gardening friend experts, I learned my soil was way too compact, allowing little drainage and oxygen."

I've made the same mistakes, stripping my gloves off, digging small holes to plop a seed that never has room enough to spread and writhe. I learned, in the clay neighborhoods of Denver, that Eko clay-buster was just going to be my heavy companion while I labored, digging up clods, sweating into the earth, getting in deep and mixing the two: old sad, dried-up souls with new vigor. The result admitted any seed, enveloped, and pushed out my ornamental horehound, my monkey flower, reaching straight up out of my dirty mind.

I needed to find other dirty minds in the search for support. That's not hard when talking to gardeners. Ross Shrigley, Senior Horticulturist at Denver Botanic Gardens, agreed with the notion that dirt can't be bought, but must be manipulated. He writes, "I know it's the soil because fresh potting soil doesn't deliver the same sensation for me. Potting soil just seems like work." He relates that when speaking to clients he tells them of " . . . the sensual feelings I have when a garden bed is prepared properly. It's digging and planting with only my hands in that bed that pushes the high until all is planted. Climax is reached when I stand back and look at it, and know what is to come."

We can be captured by dirt's call, succumb to all its earthy needs. Every spring, we are virgins anew and let our minds go deeply astray. From all outside appearances, our Lady Catherine still doesn't know what to do with that kiss on the hand, but within, there is a deep knowledge of her body. We own such knowledge now, coming back to our dirt, manipulating carnally, heaving ourselves, letting the earth dominate us until we can harvest and eat its sweet offerings.

Our acceptance, our carnal deeds don't go unrewarded. Shrigley also told me, at the end of planting, the reward of our earthen relationship, our dance, after we've let ourselves get soiled, planting beds, learning our soils, is rejoicing at earth's reward. Shrigley states, "When I prepare a bed, I imagine it as my wife describes the great sensation of shaving her legs and climbing into the clean sheets of a nicely made bed. I can easily imagine her sensation when she climbs in and I picture myself being the sheets. That's the sensation I seek when I properly prep a garden bed."

Lady Catherine would outwardly be appalled, touch her laced glove to her lips and intake breath. As the gardener is raking clods of moist earth in front of her, shirtless, a new world awakens under and inside, where she has the fantasy of rolling with him, dirt and all, in the flower bed.

References:
Dunmall, G. http://www.iconeye.com/read-previous-issues/icon-096-|-june-2011/dirt
Rice, C. http://wiredsoils.blogspot.com/2011/01/soil-is-fundamental-for-life.html
Robinson, J. http://lagunadirt.blogspot.com/

The first reviews are in!

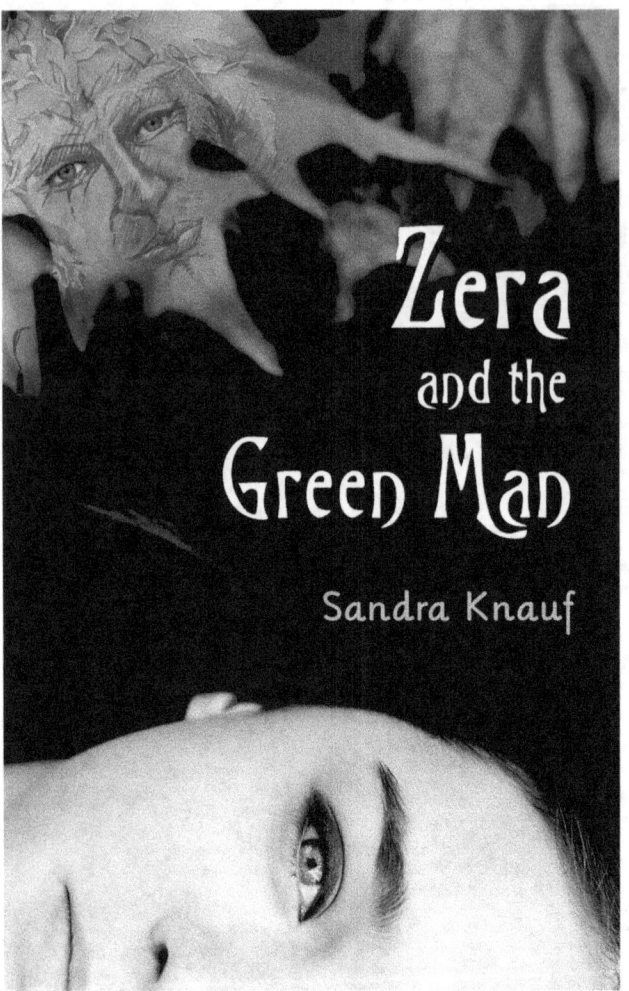

"An ambitious sci-fi novel that will charm eco-champions . . . "
–*Kirkus Reviews*

". . . . will leave readers hoping for a sequel."
–*BlueInk Review*

"The minor characters are exquisite: lively, entertaining, and complex."
–*San Francisco Book Review*

". . . one of those books that you'll want to pass on to your friends."
–Samantha Rivera for *Readers' Favorite* (five star review)

"Dairy Queen"

State Library of South Australia, 01 January 1943, via Wikimedia Commons

Leafing Through
a review of books, etc.

Sheepish: Two Women, Fifty Sheep, and Enough Wool to Save the Planet
by Catherine Friend
(Da Capo Lifelong Books, 2011)

The best books gently lead the reader to a place that gives them a different vantage point on life. The day I finished reading *Sheepish* was cool and damp, so I wound a scarf around my neck to keep warm while I sipped tea and turned pages. Then, it occurred to me—was this scarf made of wool? Yes, it was, and I appreciate my bedraggled yet still beautiful accessory more after reading this book.

Catherine Friend, whose books include *Hit by a Farm*, *The Compassionate Carnivore*, and several children's books, has written a funny, informative, sometimes sad book about her conversion from skeptical city girl to "fiber freak." Friend and her longtime partner, Melissa, follow the latter's dream to raise livestock on a Minnesota farm, but the self-described "Backup Farmer" figures out a way to find and follow her own dream.

This is a woman who jumps on the bandwagon with both feet, surprising herself by kissing lambs' heads, exploring the mystery of what makes wool "virgin," and surviving the frustrations of learning to knit: "knit one, purl two, scream three."

With charming, self-deprecating humor, Friend relates her suspicions that farming has taken her away from the life she was meant to lead. "I imagine that other people are having considerably more fun in their lives than I'm having in mine. They're dressing better, earning more, and are just more together than I am. They're going to more parties, attending more plays and movies, taking interesting classes. Their smart phones lead more interesting lives than I do."

So, of course, she turns to the virtual flora and fauna in "FarmVille" to escape the real ones outside her front door. Fortunately, that addiction doesn't last long.

Friend assures the reader that yes, life on a farm can be messy and scary, but it also can be joyful and wonderful. "Small farms like ours represent tiny pockets of enchantment, places where you can marvel at the perfect, warm eggs chickens lay. You can watch a newborn lamb stagger over to the udder and discover it for the first time. You can watch adolescent steers kick up their heels in excitement because you've come to visit them."

She's learned life lessons from the sheep, llamas, dogs, chickens, even the grapevines and alfalfa, and passes them along."A sheep can't chew her cud and run. She can't chew her cud and talk. She can't chew her cud and Twitter or e-mail or drive or exercise or really do anything but lie there and chew. I've forgotten how to do only one thing at a time, so I'm going to try harder to find a few minutes in my day when I'm not eating, talking, reading, writing, mowing, phoning, cooking, cleaning, doing chores, or stacking wood . . . to sit there not doing anything but thinking. I might feel lazy and and unproductive, but the sheep's self-esteem has remained intact, so mine should, too."

It seems unlikely that many of us would embrace a book titled *The World History of Wool*. But in Friend's skilled hands, we gladly learn that sheep's output has played pivotal roles in our culture, from the colonists' big break-up with Britain to keeping today's soldiers safe in battle. Wool and its by-products can be found in cosmetics, pianos, baseballs, crayons, ice cream, dish soap, and countless other items. Plus, it makes darn fine underwear.

So grab this book, wrap yourself in some sort of wool and enjoy the adventure. You'll be the better for it.

—*Rhonda Van Pelt*

Organic Gardener's Companion: Growing Vegetables in the West
by Jane Shellenberger
(Fulcrum Publishing, 2012)

Jane Shellenberger, publisher and editor of the much-beloved magazine *Colorado Gardener* (which she founded 15 years ago), lives and gardens on a five-acre farmette on the plains between Boulder and Longmont. Shellenberger learned about plants from her botanist mother and has been vegetable gardening in Colorado since the 1970s, after moving to Boulder as a 20 year old from Philadelphia.

Organic Gardener's Companion reads like a love letter to western gardening from a woman with 40 years of experience. Underneath the sound advice and practical steps Shellenberger weaves a strong environmental message. To her credit, she does it without preaching and yet without shying away from discussing the disastrous path we've taken during the last half-century.

She educates logically—first you learn about climate and soil. Then you educate yourself on the nutritional requirements of plants, learn about pollinators and other beneficial insects, and how to deal with "undesirables" (weeds, wildlife and unwanted insects). Being grounded in the basics is best before you actually start planting.

OGC reminded me of the heft of a Master Gardener course told as a relaxed conversation with a dear friend. The last section of the book goes into "What to Grow" describing a cornucopia of vegetables and fruits to try in the West. Shellenberger shares her personal experiences, preferences, and favorite edibles as well as friends'. Tidbits include what bush beans are delicious raw (Royalty Purple) and what strawberries are so divine that gardening friends rip their others out (Mara des Bois). I especially liked Shellenberger's ability to admit there are gaps in even her many years of experience. If there is an area where she hasn't experienced something firsthand, she says so. *OGC* is a wonderful combination of know-how and heart and the perfect primer for Western U.S. gardeners who are getting their hands dirty for the first time.
—*Sandra Knauf*

Homegrown Herbs: A Complete Guide to Growing, Using, and Enjoying More than 100 Herbs by Tammi Hartung; Photography by Saxon Holt (Storey Publishing, 2011)

Tammi Hartung's *Homegrown Herbs* is also the work of a wise Colorado plantswoman sharing a lifetime of experience in an excellent, in-depth book. Hartung, well-known around the country for her herb lectures, has been growing herbs (over 500 varieties)

with her husband in southern Colorado for over 30 years on their organic farm.

I loved how this book also covered the soil issue early ("Secrets to Great Soil") showing, as in Shellenberger's book, that this basic building block has finally been given its place at the forefront of gardening wisdom. All the nuts and bolts of herb gardening basics are covered including maintenance and pest and disease control.

This generous tome, oversized and at 255 pages is big on content. It features Saxon Holt's amazing photos of hundreds of herbs, individually and in the garden. But while it's comprehensive, it's not overwhelming. It is beautifully laid out and easy to read. I liked the yellow charts especially. They list herbs alphabetically and their specifics in regard to subjects such as Planning a Theme Garden, Herb Propagation, and Harvesting Guidelines.

An added bonus is a chapter on herbal medicines and personal care products, with recipes. Tinctures, liniments, syrups and elixirs, bath and foot soaks, insect repellents, sleep pillows, and more are explored and favorite formulas are shared. There are plenty of great sidebars like: "Liniments to Live By" which lists six herbs and where we learn "Lemon Balm will help heal cold sores," "Peppermint is soothing to sore muscles," and" Yucca will relieve joint pain." Another chapter on cooking includes Hartung's choice seasoning blends, beverages such as Mint- and Fruit-Infused Water, Hearty Vegetable Slow-Cooker Soup, Home-Baked Rosemary Bread, Licorice and Banana Oatmeal (using licorice as a sweetener—kids love it) and Early Spring Dandelion Salad.

Nearly a third of the book is devoted to "Herb Personalities." Dozens of plants and their uses, growing requirements, and even companion plantings are described with Holt's lush photos. I was surprised to find lesser-known herbs such as agastache, coyote mint, marsh mallow and motherwort featured, not to mention hollyhock, which I did not know had both medicinal uses and edible flowers!

If I could have only one book on herbs in my library it would be *Homegrown Herbs*.
—*Sandra Knauf*

Wild Flavors: One Chef's Transformative Year Cooking From Eva's Farm by Didi Emmons (Chelsea Green Publishing, 2011)

As a chef and a gardener, I was immediately attracted to *Wild Flavors*. This beautifully designed and printed (using at least 10% postconsumer recycled paper, processed chlorine free) cookbook/garden manual celebrates organic gardening, cooking, and eating seasonally. The collaboration between Boston chef Didi Emmons and organic farmer Eva Sommaripa, from Eva's Farm in Dartmouth, Massachusetts, results in a well-researched and unique cookbook that not only inspires but also visually satisfies with well-placed plant photography, recipes and the community that embraces Eva's Farm.

Written in a conversational tone with journal entries, personal stories, anecdotes, recipes, and plant profiles, Emmons gives the reader a broad view of what it means to connect fully with your garden, nature, and your community. 150 recipes range from a simple but refreshing sounding Basil Lemonade to slightly more complicated recipes including: Currant Scones with Anise Hyssop and Wild Grape Sorbet with Calaminth. Emmons relays the wisdom she received from Eva Sommaripa, farmhands, and members of her community through funny stories and life lessons on thrift, conservation, bartering and sustainability.

Starting with Winter-Salvaging and working through Spring-Community, Summer-Bartering, and Fall-Preserving the reader can glean real life examples of what it means to forage, garden and cook through the seasons. Plant profiles for 46 plants include some uncommon ones: cardoon, chickweed, and autumn olive—next to some garden favorites: basil, dill, and thyme. Emmons's in-depth plant profiles not only give the reader information about varieties but also include culinary uses, health virtues, growing, foraging, buying, storing, and prepping. As a gardener I am encouraged to add some of the more uncommon plants to my herb garden and as a chef to use what I'm currently growing to add another dimension to my seasonal recipes.

Because of Emmons's background, the cookbook is full of cooking tips, equipment suggestions, and advice designed to help readers "transform the flavors in our food." For example, in the plant profile on the herb lovage, both Emmons and Sommaripa explain how throughout the growing season lovage takes on different flavor profiles. In the spring, "tasting of celery crossed with parsley," and in the summer lovage loses most of the sweetness. Maybe because of these differences, Emmons implores readers to use her recipes as starting points and encourages creative detours.

For gardeners, cookbook enthusiasts or anyone who wants to use more locally sourced or foraged ingredients in their cooking, *Wild Flavors* will most likely change the way they think about herbs, greens, and edible "weeds."
—*Patricia Kennelly*

Small Green Roofs: Low-Tech Options for Greener Living
by Nigel Dunnett, Dusty Gedge, John Little, and Edmund C. Snodgrass (Timber Press, 2011)

Green roofs have been in use for many centuries as both an aesthetic and functional addition to buildings. The development of modern day green roofs took place primarily in Germany in the mid-to-late twentieth century, and has since become popular in cities around the world, mainly due to the environmental and economic benefits that they offer. Traditionally, these green roofs have been installed on large, flat-roofed buildings, but as the interest in green roofs has grown, green roof professionals and enthusiasts have been exploring ways to install them on virtually any type of roof whether large or small, flat or sloped. Four such individuals profile this new movement in *Small Green Roofs: Low-Tech Options for Greener Living*.

The first part of the book offers an overview of green roofs, including their purposes and myriad benefits. Also included are green roof construction basics and a very informative planting primer which covers plant selection, planting methods, maintenance considerations, and designing for wildlife. Obviously, most of this information is focused on small green roofs, and the information included was not meant to be comprehensive. For anyone seriously considering installing a green roof on their house or other buildings on their property, it is advised that they consult other sources, particularly professionals, because a poorly constructed green roof could result in major damage both to property and pocket book.

The majority of this book is filled with the profiles of 42 green roof projects broken up into 5 sections: sheds, garden offices, and studios; garages and other structures; houses; bicycle sheds and other small structures; and community projects. Each includes information on the design and planning stage, the installation process, and projects' success, along with a note by one of the authors and pictures of each project. These profiles are meant to inspire and encourage people to consider a green roof of their own and to offer ideas about how to go about it. Whether you are interested in putting a green roof on a rabbit hutch, a garden shed, or the roof of your house, this book is a great introduction to the fascinating world of green roof technology.
—*Dan Murphy*

The 50 Mile bouquet:
Seasonal, Local and
Sustainable Flowers
by Debra Prinzing;
Photography by
David E. Perry
(St. Lynn's Press, 2012)

In Praise of Chickens:
A Compendium of Wisdom
Fair and Foul
by Jane S. Smith
(Lyons Press, 2012)

I am a fresh-cut flower lover but had read enough about the floral import industry these last few years to be seriously turned off. Today's markets offer mostly imported blooms, and pesticide-drenched to boot! What's a local- and organically-grown minded girl to do?

Prinzing and Perry's book shows innovators who are answering just that question in *The 50 Mile Bouquet.* This lush offering is a compilation of real-life stories—people growing and selling sustainably- and locally-grown flowers, with growing success (pun intended), right here in the U.S.A. Perry's drool-worthy flori-porn (itself worth the price of admission) and Prinzing's prose make for a joyful combination of "We can do it!" (We're planting veggie gardens, raising backyard chickens, and now, hey, let's get slow flowers on our tables too!)

I especially liked the mentions of finding bouquet booty in your backyard, roadsides, and on public land through forest service permits—recognizing that we have an abundance right here is key. There's also a chapter about a gorgeous wedding put together with a focus on deeper meaning through hands-on participation (meaning actual work) by the bride and bridesmaids. They're out gathering fresh cut dahlias at a local farm just two days before the ceremony, and making the bouquets and aisle decorations the day of. It reminded me of my own wedding, where my mom gathered buckets of lilacs from the neighborhood. I see a better world developing here, an alternative to over-the-top expensive weddings that put the couple (or parents) into debt and which can seem more about keeping-up-with-the-Joneses than about love. D.I.Y., reveling in our own attainable "riches" and simple pleasures—oh, it does a heart good!

If there were any flaws in this gem I'd say the book is a bit narrow in scope as it deals mostly with the western United States and I wished there was a little more on backyard growers and what they can do. Those are small considerations, and books on growing your own cutting garden are not hard to find. This book inspires, and I highly recommend it to flower lovers who want to try their hand at growing or purchasing cut flowers that matter. —*Sandra Knauf*

If you're fascinated by chickens, Jane S. Smith, the award-winning author of several books (including one of my all-time favorites, *The Garden of Invention*—about Luther Burbank) has written a charming little book that will appeal to you. The book is stocking stuffer-sized (around 5" x 7") and chock-full of attractive vintage and antique illustrations. The wisdom comes largely from quotes, the wise and wry observations of both the unknown and well-known, including Aristotle, Plutarch, Pliny the Elder, Thomas Jefferson, Charles Darwin, Mark Twain, and others. Subject matter spans the obvious—from good designs for a hen house to a good ratio of rooster to hens (the answer to the second varies according to what nationality you ask!), to delicious oddities that will make you say, "Hmmm." To illustrate, I was surprised to learn that capons (castrated roosters) could be made into surrogate mothers for chicks through a strange (and rather mean) practice involving plucking their chest feathers and applying stinging nettles. It was also interesting to read about a method used a hundred years ago to preserve eggs (between 3" layers of salted butter, from the Irish).

It's all good barnyard fun, and for the chicken fancier Smith's foray into the richness of chicken lore is a great addition to the library.
—*Sandra Knauf*

Top Dressing
Dirt Poor by Cheryl Conklin

The first time I visited Laura and Tim's garden was with my friend, Kim. The evening was golden and perfectly warm. The garden rollicked over five acres of sandy soil. Once the exclusive domain of short-grass prairie and ponderosa pine, the garden billowed with color and form, so much so that I couldn't to relate to its scale and scope.

Strolling behind the house, we came upon a wilder area, bursting with hollyhocks. Beneath their rough stalks and blousey flowers, at the edge of the path, I saw black dirt peeping out from a blanket of heavy mulch. Without a thought, I crouched and thrust in my hands. Cupping the soil to my nose, I drank in its scent of life.

Behind me, Kim giggled. "You're such a farmer."

I knew she meant it as an endearment, even a compliment, but behind my heart old programming turned a rusty wheel. It was a matter of intense pride in my mother's family: We are not farmers.

If I had a ten-spot for every time I heard that proclamation while growing up in Iowa, I could easily retire. When we children really wanted to insult each other, we hurled the epithet, "Farmer!" Some boys weren't good enough to marry into the family, because they were just dumb farmers. Their kids would grow up dirt poor and become clod-hoppers like their forebears. It was a fate worse than marrying a drinker; worse, perhaps, than not marrying at all.

I can hear my mother's voice, and the voices of each of her sisters: "Shame on you!" Sometimes delivered with a chortling laugh, often as not spat, swatted, or growled at us for even minor provocations. Damning and damaging, it was a habit that soiled the soul. So often repeated, that I grew up feeling dirty.

After a Saturday night bath, one visiting aunt or another pulled on an ear. "Did you wash your neck?" Yanked from the pleasure of warm, soapy clean, the next thing I'd hear was, "Gadz, girl. Look at that. There's enough dirt on your neck to grow potatoes."

So, one of the first things I did when I broke away from them all and moved to a tiny town in northern Minnesota: I planted potatoes. I planted broccoli, carrots, beets, beans, peas, and parsnips, too.

I furrowed through the gravely loam with bare hands, making straight rows, and patting seeds gently in place. I tossed the eyed chunks of tubers into fragrant holes, mounding them every week or so as the ruddy stems climbed toward the sun. My cuticles took on a russet stain. My fingers grew coarse to the tips. My palms hummed with release as all those shameful toxins gladly sought recycling in soil.

Nearly three decades hence, in the double mitt-full cradled below my nose, my palms revel in the goodness they have found. In the dirty perfume, I taste the spuds long ago lifted from gravelly loam with naked hands.

"Thank you, Kim," I laugh, beaming up at her from the feet of the hollyhocks. "Farmer is just about the best thing anyone could call me."